HALO

HALO

Tom Maddox

A TOM DOHERTY ASSOCIATES BOOK
NEW YORK

HALO Copyright © 1991 by Tom Maddox

A Tor Book
Published by Tom Doherty Associates, Inc.
49 West 24th Street
New York, N.Y. 10010

Library of Congress Cataloging-in-Publication Data

Maddox, Tom.
      Halo / Tom Maddox.
          p.   cm.
      "A Tom Doherty Associates book."
      ISBN 0-312-85249-5
      I. Title.
    PS3563.A33946H3   1991
813'.54—dc20   91-21050
                                                                          CIP

First edition: November 1991

Printed in the United States of America

0 9 8 7 6 5 4 3 2 1

To the memory of George Maddox, my father;
Paul Cohen, my friend;
and all our lamented dead, lost in time.

CONTENTS

Part
One

Everything is destined to reappear as simulation.
—Jean Baudrillard, *America*

1

Burning, Burning

On a rainy morning in Seattle, Gonzales was ready for the egg. A week ago he had returned from Myanmar, the country once known as Burma, and now, after two days of drugs and fasting, he was prepared: he had become an alien, at home in a distant landscape.

His brain was filled with blossoms of fire, their spread white flesh torched to yellow, the center of a burning world. On the dark stained oak door, angel wings danced in blue flame, their faces beatific in the cold fire. Staring at the animated carved figures, Gonzales thought, *the fire is in my eyes, in my brain.*

He pushed down the S-curved brass handle and stepped through to the hallway, his split-toed shoes of soft cotton and rope scuffing without noise across floors of bleached oak. Through the open door at the hallway's end, morning's light through stained glass made abstract patterns of crimson and buttery yellow. Inside the room, a blue monitor console stood against the far wall, SenTrax corporate sunburst glowing on its face; in the center of the room was the egg, split hemispheres of chromed steel, cracked and waiting. One half-egg was filled with beige tubes and snakes of optic cable, the other half with hard dark plastic lying slack against the shell.

Gonzales rubbed his hands across his eyes, then pulled his hair back into a long hank and slipped a circle of elastic over it. He reached to his waist and grabbed the bottom hem of his navy blue t-shirt and pulled the shirt over his head. Dropping it to the floor, he kicked off his shoes, stepped out of baggy tan pants and loose white cotton underpants and stood naked, his pale skin gleaming with a light coat of sweat. His skin felt hot, eyes grainy, stomach sore.

He stepped up and into a chrome half-egg, then shivered and lay back as body-warmth liquid bled into the slack plastic, which began to balloon underneath him. He took hold of finger-thick cables and pushed their junction ends home into the sockets set in the back of his neck. As the egg continued to fill, he fit a mask over his face, felt its edges seal, and inhaled. Catheters moved toward his crotch, i.v. needles toward the crooks of both arms. The egg shut closed on him and liquid spilled into its interior.

He floated in silence, waiting, breathing slowly and deeply as elation punched through the chaotic mix of emotions generated by drugs, meditation, and the egg. No matter that he was going to relive his own terror, this was what moved him: access to the many-worlds of human experience—travel through space, time, and probability all in one.

Virtual realities were everywhere—virtual vacations, sex, superstardom, you name it—but compared to the egg, they were just high-res videogames or stage magic. VRs used a variety of tricks to simulate physical presence, but the sensorium could be fooled only to a certain degree, so when you inhabited a VR, you were conscious of it, so sustaining its illusion depended on willing suspension of disbelief. With the egg, however, you got total involvement through all sensory modalities—the worlds were so compelling that people waking from them often seemed lost in the waking world, as if it were a dream.

A needle punched into a membrane set in one of the neural cables and injected a neuropeptide mix. Gonzales was transported.

It was the final day of Gonzales's three week stay in Pagan, the town in central Myanmar where the government had moved its records decades earlier, in the wake of ethnic rioting in Yangon. He sat with Grossback, the Division Head of SenTrax Myanmar, at a central rosewood table in the main conference room. The table's work stations, embedded oblongs of glass, lay dark and silent in front of them.

Gonzales had come to Myanmar to do an information audit. The local SenTrax group supplied the Federated State of Myanmar with its primary information utilities: all its records of personnel and materiel, and all transactions among them. A month earlier, the local group's reports had triggered "look-see" alarms in the home company's passive auditing programs, and Gonzales and his memex had been sent to look more closely at the raw data.

So for twenty straight days Gonzales and the memex had explored data structures and their contents, testing nominal functional relationships against reality. Wherever there were movements of information, money, equipment or personnel, there were records, and the two followed. They searched cash trails, matched purchase orders to services and materiel, verified voucher signatures with personnel records, cross-checked the personnel records themselves against government databases, and traced the backgrounds and movements of the people they represented; they read contracts and back-chased to their bid and acquisition; they verified daily transaction logs.

Hard, slogging work, all patience and detail, and so far it had shown nothing but the usual inefficiencies—Grossback didn't run a particularly taut operation, but, as of the moment, he didn't seem to have a corrupt one. However, neither he nor SenTrax Myanmar was cleared yet; Gonzales's final report would come later, after he and the memex had analyzed the records at their leisure.

Gonzales stretched and rubbed his eyes. As usual at the end of short-term, intensive gigs like this, he felt tired, washed-out, eager to go. He said to Grossback, "I've got a company plane out of here late this afternoon to Bangkok. I'll connect with whatever commercial flight's available there."

Grossback smiled, obviously glad Gonzales was leaving. Grossback was a slight man, of mixed German and Thai descent; he had a light brown complexion, black hair, and delicate features. He wore clothing in the old-fashioned Burmese style: a dark skirt called a *longyi*, a white cotton shirt.

During Gonzales's time there, Grossback had dealt with him coldly and correctly from behind a mask of corporate protocol and clenched teeth. *Fair enough*, Gonzales had thought: the man's operation was suspect, and him along with it. Anyway, people routinely resented these outside intrusions; representing Internal Affairs, Gonzales answered only to his division head, F.L. Traynor, and SenTrax Board, and that made almost everyone nervous.

"You leaving out of Myaung U Airport?" Grossback asked.

"No, I've asked for a pick-up south of town." Like anyone else who could arrange it, he was not going to fly out of Pagan's official airport, where partisan groups sometimes shot down aircraft. Surely Grossback knew that.

Grossback asked, "What will your report say?"

Surprised, Gonzales said, "You know I can't tell you anything about that." Even mentioning the matter constituted an embarrassment, not to mention a reportable violation of corporate protocol. The man was either stupid or desperate.

"You haven't found anything," Grossback said.

What *was* his problem? Gonzales said, "I have a year's data to examine before I can make an assessment."

"You won't tell me what the preliminary report will look like," Grossback said. His face had gone cold.

"No," said Gonzales. He stood and said, "I have to finish packing." For the moment, he just wanted to get out before Grossback did something irretrievable, like threatening him or offering a bribe. "Goodbye," Gonzales said. The other man said nothing as Gonzales left the room.

Gonzales returned to the Thiripyitsaya Hotel, a collection of low bungalows fabricated from bamboo and ferroconcrete that stood above the Irrawaddy River. The rooms were afflicted by Myanmar's tattered version of Asian tourist decor: lacquered bamboo on the walls, along with leaping dragon holos, black teak dresser, tables, chairs, and bed frame; ceiling fans that had wandered in from the twentieth century—just to give your average citizen that rush of the Exotic East, Gonzales figured. However, the hotel had been rebuilt less than a decade before, so, by local standards, Gonzales had luxury: working climatizer, microwave, and refrigerator.

Of course, many nights the air conditioner didn't work, and Gonzales lay sweaty and semi-conscious through hot, humid nights then was greeted just after dawn by lizards fanning their ruby neck flaps and doing push-ups.

Several of those mornings he had walked the cart paths that threaded the plains around Pagan, passing among the temples and pagodas as the sun rose and turned the morning mist into a huge veil of luminous pink, with the towers sticking up like fairy castles. Everywhere around Pagan were the temples, thousands of them, young and flourishing when William the Conqueror was king. Now, quick-fab structures housing government agencies nested among thousand-year-old pagodas, some in near perfect condition, like Thatbyinnu Temple, myriad others no more than ruins and forgotten names. You gained merit by building pagodas, not by keeping up those built by someone long dead.

Like some other Southeast Asian countries, Myanmar still was trying to recover from late-twentieth century politics; in Myanmar's case, its decades-long bout with round-robin military dictatorships and the chaos that came in their wake. And as was so often the case in politically wobbly countries, it still restricted access to the worldnet; through various kinds of governments, its leaders had found the prospect of free information flow unacceptable. Ka-band antennas were expensive, their use licensed by permits almost impossible to get. As a result, Gonzales and the memex had been like meat eaters stranded among vegetarians, unable to get their nourishment.

He'd taken down the memex that morning. Its functions dormant, it lay nestled inside one of his two fiber and aluminum shock-cases, ready for transport. The other case held memory boxes containing SenTrax Myanmar group's records.

When they got home, Gonzales would tell the memex the latest news about Grossback, how the man had cracked at the last moment. Gonzales was sure what the m-i would think of what he did—Grossback was dog dirty and scared they would find it.

❖   ❖   ❖

At the edge of a sandy field south of Pagan, Gonzales waited for his plane. He wore his usual international traveler's mufti, a tan gabardine two-piece suit over an open-collared white linen shirt, dark brown slipover shoes. His hair was gathered back into a ponytail held together by a silver ring made from lizard figures joined head-to-tail. Next to him sat a soft brown leather bag and the two shock-cases.

In front of him a pagoda climbed in a series of steeples to a gilded and jeweled umbrella top, pointing to heaven. On its steps, beside the huge paw of a stone lion, a monk sat in full lotus, his face shadowed by the animal rising massive and lumpy and mock fierce above him. The lion's flanks were dyed orange by sunset, its lips stained the color of dried blood. The minutes passed, and the monk's voice droned, his face in shadow.

"Come tour the temples of ancient Pagan," a voice said. "Shwezigon, Ananda, Thatbyinnu—"

"Go away," Gonzales said to the tour cart that had rolled up behind him. It would hold two dozen or so passengers in eight rows of narrow wooden benches but was now empty—almost all the tourists would have joined the crush on the terraces of Thatbyinnu, where they could watch the sun set over the temple plain.

"Last tour of the day," the cart said. "Very cheap, also very good exchange rate offered as courtesy to visitors."

It wanted to exchange kyats for dollars or yen: in Myanmar, even the machines worked the black market. "No thanks."

"Extremely good rate, sir."

"Fuck off," Gonzales said. "Or I'll report you as defective." The cart whirred as it moved away.

Gonzales watched a young monk eyeing him from the other side of the road, ready to come across and beg for pencils or money. Gonzales caught the monk's eye and shook his head. The monk shrugged and walked on, his orange robe billowing.

Where the hell was his plane? Soon hunter flares would cut into the new moon's dark, and government drones would scurry around the edges of the shadows like huge mutant bats. Upcountry Myanmar trembled on the edge of chaos, beset by a multi-ethnic mix of Karens, Kachins, and Shans in various political postures, all fierce, all contemptuous of the central government. They fought with whatever was at hand, from sharpened stick to backpack missile, and they quit only when they died.

A high-pitched wail built quickly until it filled the air. Within seconds a silver swing-wing, an ungainly thing, each huge rectangular wing loaded with a bulbous, oversized engine pod, came low over the dark mass of forest. Its running lights flashing red and yellow, the swing-wing slewed to a stop above the field, wings tilting to the perpendicular and engine sound dropping into the bass. Its spots picked out a ten-meter circle of white light that the aircraft dropped into, blowing clouds of sand that swept over Gonzales in a whirlwind. The inverted fans' roar dropped to a whisper, and with a creak the plane kneeled on its gear, placing the cockpit almost on the ground. Gonzales picked up his bags and walked toward the plane. A ladder unfolded with a hydraulic hiss, and Gonzales stepped up and into the plane's bubble.

"Mikhail Gonzales?" the pilot asked. His multi-function flight glasses were tilted back on his forehead, where their mirrored ovoid lenses made a blank second pair of eyes; a thin strand of black fiberoptic cable trailed from their rim. Beneath the glasses, his thin face was brown and seamed— *no cosmetic work for this guy,* Gonzales thought. The man wore a throwaway "tropical" shirt with dancing pink flamingos on a navy blue background.

"That's me," Gonzales said. He gestured with the shock-case in his right hand, and the pilot toggled a switch that opened the luggage locker. Gonzales put his bags into the steel compartment and watched as the safety net pulled tight against the bags and the compartment door closed. He took a seat in the first of eight empty rows behind the pilot. Cushions sighed beneath him, and from the seatback in front of him a feminine voice said, "You should engage your harness. If you need instructions, please say so now."

Gonzales snapped closed the trapezoidal catch where shoulder and lap belts connected, then stretched against the harness, feeling the sweat dry on his skin in the plane's cool interior. "Thank you," said the voice.

The pilot was speaking to Myaung U Airport traffic control as the plane lifted into twilight over the city. The soft white glow from the dome light vanished, then there were only the last moments of orange sunlight coming through the bubble.

The temple plain was spread out beneath, all murk and shadow, with the temple and pagoda spires reaching up toward the light, white stucco and gold tinted red and orange.

"Man, that's a beautiful sight," the pilot said.

"You're right," Gonzales said. It was, but he'd seen it before, and besides, it had already been a long day.

The pilot flipped his glasses down, and the plane banked left and headed south along the river. Gonzales lay back in his seat and tried to relax.

They flew above black water, following the Irrawaddy River until they crossed an international flyway to Bangkok. Dozing in the interior darkness, Gonzales was almost asleep when he heard the pilot say, "Shit, somebody's here. Partisan attack group, probably—no recognition codes. Must be flying ultralights—our radar didn't see them. We've got an image now, though."

"Any problem?" Gonzales asked.

"Just coming for a look. They don't bother foreign charters." And he pointed to their transponder message flashing above the primary displays:

THIS INTERNATIONAL FLIGHT IS NON-MILITARY.
IT CLAIMS RIGHT OF PASSAGE
UNDER U.N. ACT OF 2020.

It would keep on repeating until they crossed into Thai airspace.

The flight computer display lit bright red with **COLLISION WARNING,** and a Klaxon howl filled the plane's interior. The pilot said, "Fuck, they launched!" The swing-wing's turbines screamed full out as the plane's computer took command, and the pilot's hands gripped his yoke, not guiding, just hanging on.

Gonzales's straps pulled tight as the plane tumbled and fell, corkscrewed, looped, climbed again—smart metal fish evading fiery harpoons. Explosions blossomed in the dark, quick asymmetrical bursts of flame followed immediately by hard thumping sounds and shock waves that knocked the swing-wing as it followed its chaotic path through the night.

Then an ultralight appeared, flaring in fire that surged around it, its pilot in blazing outline—a stick figure with arms thrown to the sky in the instant before pilot and aircraft disintegrated in flame.

Their own flight went steady and level, and control returned to the pilot's yoke. Gonzales's shocked retinas sparkled as the night returned to blackness. "Collision averted," the plane's computer said. "Time in red zone, six point eight nine seconds."

"What the hell?" Gonzales said. "What happened?"

"Holy Jesus motherfucker," the pilot said.

Gonzales sat gripping his seat, chilled by the blast of cold air from the plane's air conditioner onto his sweat-soaked shirt. He glanced down to his lap: no, he hadn't pissed himself. Really, everything happened too quickly for him to get *that* scared.

A Mitsubishi-McDonnell "Loup Garou" warplane dived in front of them and circled in slow motion. Like the ultralights it was cast in matte black, but with a massive fuselage. It made a slow barrel roll as it circled them, lazy predator looping fat, slow prey, then turned on brilliant floods that played across their canopy.

The pilot and Gonzales both froze in the glare.

Then the Loup Garou's black cockpit did a reverse-fade; behind the transparent shell Gonzales saw the mirror-visored pilot, twin cables running from the base of his neck. The Loup Garou's wings slid forward into reverse-sweep, and it stood on its tail and disappeared.

Gonzales strained against his taut harness.

"Assholes!" the pilot screamed.

"Who was that?" Gonzales asked, his voice thin and shaking. "What do you mean?"

"The Myanmar Air Force," the pilot said, his voice tight, face red beneath the flight glasses' mirrors. "They set us up, the pricks. They used us to troll for a guerrilla flight." The pilot flipped up his glasses and stared with pointless intensity out the cockpit window, as if he could see through the blackness. "And waited," he said. "Waited till they had the whole flight." The pilot swiveled around abruptly and faced Gonzales, his features distorted into a mad and angry caricature of the man who had welcomed Gonzales ninety minutes before. "Do you know how fucking close we came?" he asked.

No, Gonzales shook his head. *No.*

"Milliseconds, man. Fucking milliseconds. Close enough to touch," the pilot said. He swiveled his seat to face forward, and Gonzales heard its locking mechanism click as he settled back into his own seat, fear and shame spraying a wild neurochemical mix inside his brain—

Gonzales had never felt things like this before—death down his spine and up his gut, up his throat and nose, as close as his skin; death with a bad smell . . . *burning, burning.*

2

Anything I Can Do to Help You

As the morning passed, the sun moved away from the stained glass, and the room's interior went to gloom. Only monitor lights remained lit, steady rows of green above flickering columns of numbers on the light blue face of the monitor panel.

A housekeeping robot, a beige pod the size of a large goose, worked slowly across the floor, nuzzled into the room's corners, then left the room, its motion tentacles beneath it making a sound like wind through dry grass.

The cockpit display flashed as landing codes fed through the flight computer, then the swing-wing locked into the Bangkok landing grid and began its slide down an invisible pipe. They went to touchdown guided by electronic hands.

The pilot turned to Gonzales as they descended and said, "I'll have to file a report on the attack. But you're lucky—if we had landed in Myanmar, government investigators would have been on you like white on rice, and then you could forget about leaving for days, maybe weeks. You're okay now: by the time they process the report and ask the Thais to hold you, you'll be gone."

At the moment, the last thing Gonzales wanted to do was spend any time in Myanmar. "I'll get out as quickly as I can," he said.

Now that it was all over, he could feel the fear climbing in him like the onset of a dangerous drug. Trying to calm himself, he thought, *really, nothing happened, except you got the shit scared out of you, that's all.*

As the swing-wing settled on the pad, Gonzales stood and went to pick up his luggage from the open baggage hold. The pilot sat watching as the plane went through its shutdown procedures.

Do something, Gonzales said to himself, feeling panic mount. He pulled the memex's case out of the hold and said, "I want a copy of your flight records."

"I can't do that."

"You can. I'm working with Internal Affairs, and I was almost killed while flying in your aircraft."

"So was I, man."

"Indeed. But I need this data. Later, IA will go the full official route and pick everything up, but I need it now. A quick dump into my machine here, that's all it will take. I'll give you authorization and receipt." Gonzales waited, keeping the pressure on by his insistent gaze and posture.

The pilot said, "Okay, that ought to cover my ass."

Gonzales slid the shock-case next to the pilot's seat, kneeled and opened the lid. "Are you recording?" he asked the pilot.

The man nodded and said, "Always."

"That's what I thought. All right, then: for the record, this is Mikhail Mikhailovitch Gonzales, senior employee of Internal Affairs Division, SenTrax. I am acquiring flight records of this aircraft to assist in my investigation of certain events that occurred during its most recent flight." He looked at the pilot. "That should do it," he said.

He pulled out a data lead from the case and snapped it into the access plug on the instrument panel. Lights flashed across the panel as data began to spool into the quiescent memex. The panel gonged softly to signal transfer was complete, and Gonzales unplugged the lead and closed the case. "Thanks," he said to the pilot, who sa, staring out the cockpit bubble.

Gonzales stood and patted the case and thought to himself, *hey, memex, got a surprise for you when you wake up.* He felt much better.

A carry-slide hauled Gonzales a mile or so through a brightly-lit tunnel with baby blue plastic and plaster walls marked with signs in half a dozen languages promising swift retribution for vandalism. Red and green virus graffiti smeared everything, signs included, and as Gonzales watched, messages in Thai and Burmese transmuted, and new stick figures emerged with dialogue balloons saying god knows what. A lone phrase in red paint read in English, HEROIN ALPHA DEVIL FLOWER. Shattered boxes of black fibroid or coarse sprays of multiwire cable marked where surveillance cameras had been.

Grey floor-to-ceiling steel shutters blocked the narrow portal to International Arrivals and Departures. Faceless holoscan robots—dark, wheeled cubes with carbon-fiber armor and tentacles and spiked sensor antennas—worked the crowd, antennas swiveling.

All around were Asian travelers, dark-suited men and women: Japanese, Chinese, Malaysians, Indonesians, Thai. They spread out from Asia's "dragons," world centers of research and manufacturing, taking their low margins and hard sell to Europe and the Americas, where

17

consumption had become a way of life. Everywhere Gonzales traveled, it seemed, he found them: cadres armed with technical and scientific prowess and fueled by persistent ambition.

They formed the steel core of much of the world's prosperity. The United States and the dragons lived in uneasy symbiosis: the Asians had a hundred ways of making sure the American economy didn't just roll over and die and take the prime North American consumer market with it. Whether Japanese, Koreans, Taiwanese, Hong Kong Chinese-Canadians—they bought some corporations and merged with others, and Americans ended up working for General Motors Fanuc, Chrysler Mitsubishi, or Daewoo-Dec, and with their paychecks they bought Japanese memexes, Korean autos, Malaysian robotics.

Shutter blades cranked open with a quick scream of metal, and Gonzales stepped inside. An Egyptian guard in a white headdress, blue-and-white checked headband, and gray U.N. drag, cross-checked his ID, gave a quick, meaningless smile—teeth white and perfect under a black moustache—and waved him on.

Southeast Asian Faction Customs waited in the form of a small Thai woman in a brown uniform with indecipherable scrawls across yellow badges. Her features were pleasant and impassive; she wore her black hair pulled tightly back and held with a clear plastic comb. She stood behind a gray metal table; on the floor next to it was a two-meter-high general purpose scanner, its controls, screens, and read-outs hidden under a black cloth hood. Dirty green walls wore erratically spaced signs in a dozen languages, detailing in small type the many categories of contraband.

The woman motioned for him to sit in the upright chair in front of the table, then for him to put his clothes bag and cases on the table.

She spoke, and the translator box at her waist echoed in clear, neuter machine English: "Your person has been scanned and cleared." She put the soft brown bag into the mouth of the scanner, and the machine vetted the bag with a quiet beep. The woman slid it back to Gonzales.

She spoke again, and the translator said, "Please open these cases," as she pointed toward the two shock-cases. For each, Gonzales screened the access panel with his left hand and tapped in the entry codes with his right. The case lids lifted with a soft sigh. Inside the cases, monitor and diagnostic lights flashed above rows of memory modules, heavy solids of black plastic the size of a small safety deposit box.

Gonzales saw she was holding a copy of the Data Declaration Form the memex had filled out in Myanmar and transmitted to both Myanmar and Thai governments. She looked into one of the cases and pointed to a row of red-tagged and sealed memory modules.

The translator's words followed behind hers and said, "These modules we must hold to verify that they contain no contraband information."

"Myanmar customs did so. These are SenTrax corporate records."

"Perhaps they are. We have not cleared them."

"If you wish, I will give you the access protocols. I have nothing to hide, but the modules are important to my work."

She smiled. "I do not have proper equipment. They must be examined by authorities in the city." The translator's tones accurately reflected her lack of concern.

Gonzales sensed the onset of severe bureaucratic intransigence. For whatever occult reasons, this woman had decided to fuck him around, and the harder he pushed, the worse things would be. Give it up, then. He said, "I assume they will be returned to me as soon as possible."

19

"Certainly. After careful examination. Though it is unlikely that the examination can be completed before your departure." She slid the case off her desk and to the floor behind it. She was smiling again, a satisfied bureaucrat's smile. She turned back to her console, Gonzales's case already a thing of the distant past. She looked up to see him still standing there and said, "How else can I help you?"

The machine-world began to disperse, turning to fog, and as it did, banks of low-watt incandescents lit up around the room's perimeter, and the patterns of console lights went through a series of rapid permutations as Gonzales was brought to a waking state. The room's lights had been full up for an hour when the desynching series was complete and the egg began to split.

Inside the egg Gonzales lay pale, nude, near-comatose, machine-connected: a new millennium Snow White. A flesh-colored catheter led from his water-shrunken genitals, transparent i.v. feeds from both forearms. White sealant and anti-irritant paste had clotted around the tubes from throat and mouth. The sharp ozone smell of the paste was all over him.

An autogurney had rolled next to the egg, and its hands, shining chrome claws, began disconnecting tubes and leads. Then it worked with hands and black flexible arms the thickness of a stout rope to lift Gonzales from the egg and onto its own surface.

Gonzales woke up in his own bedroom and began to whimper. "It's okay," the memex whispered through the room's speaker. "It's okay."

Some time later Gonzales awoke again, lay in gloom and considered his condition. Some nausea, legs weak, but no apparent loss of gross motor control, no immediate parapsychological effects (disorientations, amnesias, synesthesias) . . .

Gonzales got up and went to the bathroom, stood amid white tile, polished aluminum and mirrors and said, "Warm shower." Water hissed, and the shower stall door swung open. The water ran down his skin and the sweat and paste rolled off his body.

3

Dancing in the Dark

The next morning, Gonzales stood looking out his front window, down Capitol Hill to the city and the bay. After a full night's sleep, he felt recovered from the egg. Halfway down the hill stood a row of Contempo high-rises—half a dozen shapes in the mist, their sides laced with optic fiber in patterns of red, blue, white, and yellow.

From the wallscreen behind him, a voice said, "The Fine Arts Network, showing today only: the legendary 'Rothschild Ads—Originals and Copies,' a Euro/Com Production from the Cannes Festival; also showing, NipponAuto's 'Ecstasy for Many Kilometers.'"

"Cycle," Gonzales said. He turned to watch as the screen split into windows, showing eight at a time in a random-access search. In the screen's upper-right corner, the Headline Service cycled what it considered important: worsening social collapse in England; another series of politico-economic triumphs for The Two Koreas. And the

Ecostate Summaries: ozone hole #2 over the Antarctic conforming to predicted self-repair curve, hole #3 obstinately holding steady; CO_2 portions unstable, ozone reaching for an ugly part of the graph; temperature fluctuations continuing to evade best predictions . . .

Why call it *news?* wondered Gonzales. Call it *olds.* Christ, this stuff had been going on forever, it seemed . . .

He said, "Memex, what do you think about the attack?"

"A bad business," said the memex. "We are lucky to have survived." It seemed a bit subdued in the aftermath of the trip in the egg, as though it, too, had come close to dying. Gonzales didn't know how it experienced such things, given its limited sensory modalities and, he presumed, lack of a fear of death.

"What's happening in the real world?" Gonzales asked.

"Your mother left a message for you. Do you want to look at it now?"

"Might as well."

On the screen she lay back in a lawn chair, her face hidden behind a sun mask, her mono-bikinied body a rich brown. She sat up and said, "Still in Myanmar, huh, sweetie? When are you coming back? I'd love to talk, but I just won't pay those rates."

She removed her sun mask. She had dark skin and good bones; her face was nearly unlined, though her skin had the faint parchment quality of age. Her small breasts sagged very little. Body and face, she appeared an athletic fifty year old who had perhaps seen too much sun. She would turn eighty-seven next month.

Since Gonzales's father had died in a flash flu epidemic while the two were visiting Naples, his mother had turned her energies and interests to maintaining her health and appearance. Half the year she spent in Cozumel's Regeneration Villas, where tissue transplants and genetic retailor-

23

ing kept her young. The rest of the time she occupied an entire floor of a low-res condo on Florida's decaying Gold Coast, just north of Ciudad de Miami. Top dollar, but she could afford it.

She and his father had been charter members of the gerontocracy, that ever-expanding league of the rich and old who vied with the young for their society's resources. The young had the strength and energy of youth; the old had wealth, power and cunning. No contest: kids under thirty often stated their main life's goal as "living until I am old enough to enjoy it."

Gonzales's mother draped a blue-and-white print cotton robe over her shoulders and said, "Call me. I'll be home in a week or so. Be well."

Their talks, her taped messages—both usually made him feel baffled and angry—but today her self-absorption pricked sharper than usual. *I almost died,* he wanted to tell her, *they almost killed me, mother.*

But he was far away from her, as far as Seattle was from Miami. *And whose fault is that?* a small voice asked. He had chosen to come here, as distant from southern Florida as he could get and remain in the continental United States. Sometimes he felt he'd come a bit too far. In Florida, people cooled down with alcohol in iced drinks; here, they warmed their chilly selves with strong coffee. Gonzales often felt lost among the glum and health-conscious Northerners and craved the Hispanic sensuality and demonstrativeness of southern Florida.

Still, how he hated the world he'd grown up in. He had seen the movers, dealers, and players since he was a child, and in all of them he had felt the same obsessive grasping at money and land and power and had heard the same childish voices, wanting *more more more.* At his parents' parties, he remembered dark southern Florida faces—sunburned whites, blacks, Hispanics; men with heavy gold

jewelry, trailing clouds of expensive cologne, and women with stiff hair and pushed-up breasts whose laughter made brittle footnotes to the men's loud voices. He'd fled all that as instinctively as a child yanks its hand from a fire.

Both there and here he stood in an alien land, no more at home at one end of the country than the other.

"No reply," Gonzales said.

The next day Gonzales sat in the solarium, where he lounged among black lacquer and etched glass while thoughts of death gnawed at the edges of his torpor. He filled a bronze pipe with small green sensemilla leaves and holed up in a haze of smoke and drank tea.

The late afternoon light through the windows went to pure Seattle Gray, the color of ennui and unemphatic despair, and his solitude became oppressive. He needed company, he thought, and wondered what it would be like to have a cat. Then he thought about the truth of it, how often he would be gone and the cat left to itself and the house's machines. "Here kitty kitty," the cleaning robot would say, and the memex would want veterinary programs and a diagnostic link . . . fuck it, they all could live without a cat.

Then a hunger kick came on him, and he decided to make taboulleh. "You are not taking care of business," the memex said to Gonzales as he stood chopping mint leaves, green onions and tomato, squeezing lemon and stirring in bulgur wheat with the patience of the deeply stoned.

"True," Gonzales said. "I'm in no hurry."

"Why not?"

"I'm going to die, my friend." The smells of lemon and mint drifted up to him, and he inhaled them deeply. He said, "Today, mañana, some day for sure . . . and I'm still trying to understand what that means to me *now*. To be productive, that is fine, but to come to terms with my own

mortality . . . I think that is better." The taboulleh was
finished. It was beautiful; he wanted to rub his face in it.

Not long after he finished eating, a package arrived from
Thailand. Inside layers of foam and strapping were the
memory modules the Thais had taken. When he plugged
the modules into the memex, they showed empty: zeroed,
ready to be used again.

Gonzales stood looking at the racked modules in the
memex closet. *I can't fucking believe it,* he thought. In
effect, the audit had been canceled out. Whatever data he
or anyone else collected at this point from SenTrax Myanmar would be essentially useless, Grossback having been
given time to cook the data if he needed to do so. A fatal
indeterminacy had settled on the whole affair.

Grossback, you bastard, thought Gonzales. *If you arranged for the Thais to grab these boxes, maybe you are
smarter and meaner than I thought.*

"Shit," Gonzales said.

"Is there anything I can do?" the memex asked.

"Nothing I can think of."

From the background of jungle plants and pastel walls
and the signature pieces of curved silver, HeyMex recognized the latest incarnation of the Beverly Rodeo Hotel's
public lounge. Mister Jones preferred ostentation, even in
simulacra.

HeyMex settled into a sling chair made of bright chrome
and stuffed chocolate-brown leather. HeyMex wore the
usual baggy pants and jacket of black cotton, a crumpled
white linen shirt; was smooth-faced and had close-cropped
hair.

A figure shimmered into being in the chair opposite:
silver suit and red metal-laced shirt brilliant under lights;

black-framed glasses with dark lenses; greased hair combed straight back, a little black goatee and moustache.

"Mister Jones," HeyMex said.

The other figure took a long, slow drag off a brown cigarette. "HeyMex," it said. "What can I do for you?"

"It's Gonzales. Since we got back from Myanmar, he's been passive, hasn't been taking care of business."

"Post-trauma response—give him some time, he'll be okay."

"No, he doesn't need time. He needs work. Have you got something?"

"Maybe. I haven't run a personnel search—he might not fit the exact profile."

"Never mind that. Give it to Gonzales. He needs it."

"If you say so. You'll hear something official later today."

The world went translucent, then turned to smoke, and Mister Jones disappeared back into his identity as Traynor's advisor, HeyMex into his as Gonzales's memex.

(Ask yourself why the two machines chose this elaborate masquerade, or why no one knew these sorts of things were happening. However, as to the *who?* and the *why?* there can be no question. These are the new players, and these are their games.

So welcome to the new millennium.)

4

Privileged Not to Exist

When Gonzales returned home, he found a message from Traynor: "Will arrange for transportation tomorrow morning, five A.M., from Northern Seattle Airtrack to my estate. Be prepared for immediate work. Pack the memex and twenty-two kilos personal luggage."

"Shit," Gonzales said. "We just got home. Twenty-two kilos, huh? That means we'll be going . . . where do you think?"

The memex said, "Somewhere in orbit."

The airport limo held its spot in a locked sequence of a dozen vehicles moving away from the city at two hundred kilometers an hour. Seattle's northern suburbs showed as patches of light behind shifting mist and steady-falling rain. Overhead, cargo blimps flying toward Vancouver moved through the clouds like great coldwater fish.

Gonzales got a quick view of a square where white and

yellow searchlights played across a concrete landscape, and a gangling assemblage of pipe and wire stepped crab-wise as it sprayed a brick wall: a graffiti robot, a machine built and set loose to scrawl messages to the world at large. Gonzales could only read GENT OF CHAN . . .

With a sigh from its turbines, the limo slowed to exit into North Seattle Airtrack, then turned into the private-field access road. A wire gate opened in front of them as it received the codes the limo sent. Near the SenTrax hangar waited a swing-wing exactly like the one that had taken Gonzales from Pagan to Bangkok. Gonzales climbed into the plane, placed his bag and the memex's shock-cases into the plane's baggage locker, seated himself, and pulled his shoulder harness tight.

The swing-wing rose into clouds and fog. The blank whiteness out the windows and steady noise of the swing-wing's engines lulled Gonzales into a light sleep that lasted until the ascending scream of engine noise told him they were landing.

As the plane tilted, Gonzales saw the blue sheet of Lake Tahoe stretching away to the south, then a patch of green lawn on the water's edge that grew bigger as the swing-wing made its final approach to Traynor's estate.

From his six years' work with Internal Affairs, the past two as independent auditor, Gonzales knew quite a bit about Frederick Lewis Traynor, his boss. Traynor had wealth sufficient for even the most extravagant tastes—it was his family's, and he had known nothing else—but power whose smallest touch could shape lives, imprint stone, that he longed for. From his position as head of Internal Affairs, one of SenTrax's most powerful divisions, he plotted ascent to the SenTrax Board; he wanted to be one of the twenty people who had moved beyond negotiation and compromise, whose desires were reality, whims action.

In fact, Traynor had already achieved a level of eminence that is privileged, when it wishes, not to exist. His house and land occupied a chunk of the North Shore of Lake Tahoe where there had once been two casino-hotels and a section of state highway. The hotels had been demolished, the highway diverted. The grounds were now surrounded by a four-meter-high fence of slatted black steel—alarmed, hotwired, and robot-patrolled. The estate showed on no map or record of purchase, ownership or taxation; neither did the man himself.

When Gonzales stepped out of the plane onto a great expanse of green lawn, Traynor waited to meet him. He was short and pudgy, and his skin was pale. His sparse hair lay limp in dark curls on his skull. On his feet were soft black slippers, and he wore an embroidered silk robe— green and blue and white and red, with rearing dragons across back and front. He thought of himself as Byronic— eccentric and interesting, afflicted by genius—but to Gonzales and many others he appeared simply petulant and self-indulgent.

Traynor stretched his arms wide and said, "Mikhail," giving the name three syllables, saying it right, then took Gonzales in a brief hug. Traynor then stood back and looked at him and said, "You don't look too bad."

"Is that why you brought me here, to look at me?"

Traynor shrugged. "For that, maybe, and to talk to you about your next job. Besides, I like you."

Gonzales supposed that Traynor did like him, in his peculiar boss's and rich man's way. Particularly, he seemed to like the fact that Gonzales wasn't awed by the outward and visible manifestations of his money and power.

"Good breeding," Traynor had said to him once. "That's your secret: patrician and plebeian blood mixed." Mikhail Mikhailovitch Gonzales was of mixed blood indeed; among others, Russian Jews and Hispanics from Los Angeles on

30

his mother's side, blacks from Chicago and Cubans from Miami on his father's. Among his family background were slaves and field workers and bourgeois counter-revolutionaries, along with the odd artist and smuggler and con man.

However, whatever his breeding or experience, he had to put up with lots of cheerful, condescending bullshit from Traynor, as he had to put up with Traynor in general, because the man *was* rich and powerful and the boss, and neither of them ever forgot it.

The two walked toward the house that stood facing the lake at the lawn's far border, a Stately Home an idealized eighteenth-century English architect might have built for an equally idealized and indulgent patron. Off a golden domed center stood three wings of creamy stone, the whole in restrained neo-Palladian with no modern excesses of material, no foamed colored concrete and composites, just the tan and creamy sandstone and rose marble speaking wealth and taste.

They climbed up marble stairs and passed into the house and under a looming interior dome that soared high above the central rotunda where the house's three wings joined. They walked down a hallway of dark wainscoting below cream walls and ceiling.

Gonzales caught glimpses of side rooms through open doorways as they passed. One room appeared to front upon a night filled with swirling nebulae and a million stars, the enxt on sunshine and dazzling snows. Still another contained nothing but white walls, floors of polished marble and a five-meter hand centered motionless in midair—index finger extended, other three fingers curled against the palm, thumb erect on top like the hammer of a make-believe gun.

Mahogany doors parted in front of the two men, and they passed into the library. Its dark-paneled walls gave away nothing: even close up, the books might have been holo-fronts, might have been real. Flat data entry modules were laid into mahogany side tables that stood next to red leather easy chairs and maroon velour couches.

"Sit down, Mikhail," Traynor said.

Gonzales could feel the silence heavy and somber among the dark invocations of another time, leather and furnishings conjuring up men's clubs, smoking rooms, the somber whispers of deals going down.

Traynor's eyes lost focus as he went rapt, listening to his voice within. Even if he hadn't been aware of Traynor's dependence on his advisor, Gonzales would have known what was happening. Traynor, higher up in the executive food chain than anyone else of Gonzales's acquaintance, needed permanent real-time access to the information, advice, and general emotional support his advisor supplied, so Traynor was wired with a bone-set transceiver just under his left ear. Wherever he went, his advisor's voice went with him, through cellular networks and satellite links.

Traynor finally looked up and said, "Look, I want you to get focused on a job you're going to do for me. Can you do that?" Gonzales shrugged. Traynor said, "You're upset and angry—you were attacked, almost killed—I know that. But look: you work for Internal Affairs, it's an occupational hazard. You and your machine poked hard at this man's operation, and you spooked him, so he did something stupid."

"And I want to make him pay for it."

"You play along with me on this one, and maybe you'll be able to. But later—now I've got other work for you."

"Okay, if you wish." Gonzales knew his only chance to even things up with Grossback was to lay low now, pay back later.

"Good," Traynor said. "How much do you know about Halo City and Aleph?"

"The city was put together by a multi-national consortium. SenTrax has a data monopoly, employs a large-scale m-i to administer the city. That's about all I know."

The wallscreen at one end lit up with a glyph in hard black:

$$\aleph_0$$

The voice of Traynor's advisor spoke through a ceiling speaker; it said, "The sign you are looking at is the original emblem of the Aleph system when it was built by SenTrax. In Cantor's notation, it represents the first of the transfinite numbers—denoting the infinite set of integers and fractions, or natural numbers. Aleph is also the first letter of the Hebrew alphabet and the name of a story—"

"Get on with it," Traynor said.

"The system was constructed at Athena Station, in geo-synchronous orbit, where it supervised the construction of the Orbital Energy Grid, and later was transported to Halo City, at L5, where it serves as the primary agent of data interpretation, logistical planning, and administration."

Gonzales said, "Seems odd to have a project the size and importance of Halo administered by an obsolete m-i."

"It would be so if Aleph were obsolete," answered the advisor. "However, this is not the case. The machine we refer to as Aleph, has capabilities superior to any existing m-i."

Gonzales looked at Traynor, who held up a hand, indicating *have patience*, and said, "Next series."

On the screen came a pan shot across a weightless space where a man floated, encased in a transparent plastic bubble. He was naked, and his limbs were shrunken and twisted. He had tubes in his nose, mouth, ears, penis, and anus, metal cups over his eyes. Two thick cables connected to junctions at the back of his neck.

The advisor said, "This man's name is Jerry Chapman.

He suffers from severe neural damage, the results of a toxin transmitted through seafood contaminated with toxic waste. Though most motor and sensory functions are disabled, he is not comatose. In fact, he appears to retain all intellectual function. Note the neural interface sockets: they are the key to what follows."

"He's at Halo?" Gonzales asked.

"Yes," the advisor said. "He was taken there from Earth."

"Very special treatment," Gonzales said.

"The group at Halo has been looking for such an opportunity," the advisor said. "To explore long-term Aleph-interface."

Traynor said, "In fact, Chapman's relations with Aleph go back to the machine's early days."

The advisor said, "When he and Aleph worked with Doctor Diana Heywood, who at the time was employed by SenTrax at Athena Station. She was blind at that time."

"Even in this deck, Doctor Heywood's the joker," Traynor said. "She was involved with Aleph at the time, and later she lived with Chapman, on Earth. She was released by SenTrax for unauthorized use of the Aleph system, but we've brought her back into our employ. She's going to Halo, where she will assist Aleph in an attempt to keep this man alive."

"Alive?" Gonzales asked, gesturing toward the hulk on the screen. "There doesn't seem much point." As he understood these things, given the man's condition, withdrawal processing should have started, SenTrax as medical guardians making application to the Federal Medical Courts for permission to cease support.

The advisor said, "Aleph believes it can keep him alive in machine-space. There are special problems, as you can imagine, among them the need to have love, friendship . . . I do not understand these matters well, but Aleph has communicated to me that the next weeks are critical for the patient."

Traynor said, "However, using Doctor Heywood presents its own problems."

"She left SenTrax years ago," the advisor said. "In somewhat strained circumstances."

Traynor said, "So she has no reason to be loyal to the company." He paused. "And we have no reason to trust her."

Gonzales said, "I presume this is where I enter in?"

"Yes," Traynor said. "I want you to accompany her. You will represent me and, indirectly, SenTrax Board." Gonzales raised his eyebrows, and Traynor laughed. "Yes, I am representing the board on this one, unofficially—they see this treatment as being of enormous interest but wish to have a certain insulation between them and these matters, given that certain tricky legal issues will have to be skirted."

"Or trampled on," said Gonzales.

"As you wish," said Traynor. "The important point is this: from the board's point-of-view, Doctor Heywood cannot be trusted."

Gonzales said, "So you need a spy, and I'm it."

Traynor shrugged.

The advisor said, "You represent properly vested interests in a situation where they would not otherwise be adequately represented."

Gonzales said, "That's a good one, 'represent properly vested interests.' I'll try to remember it. Okay, I'll do my best." He turned to face Traynor and said, "To get you on the board." Traynor laughed. Gonzales asked, "How long will this thing take?"

"Not too long," Traynor said.

The advisor said, "Once Chapman's state has been stabilized—"

"Or he dies," Traynor said.

"Highly probable," said the advisor. "Once he is stable—alive or dead—your job will be finished."

Traynor said, "But until then, your job is to let me know what's happening. You'll be in machine-space along with them, and you'll see what they're doing."

"Fine," Gonzales said. "So what do I do now?"

"You fly to Berkeley and talk to Doctor Heywood," Traynor said. "Introduce yourself. Make a friend."

5

So Come to Me, Then

Gonzales arrived at Berkeley Aeroport, a collection of cracked cement pads at the edge of the water, by midafternoon. He stepped out of the swing-wing into blazing sunshine. Across the bay, the Golden Gate and Alcatraz Island danced in the glare; the water glittered so intensely his sunglasses went nearly black.

A Truesdale rental waited for him in the parking lot. He stuck a SenTrax ID/credit chip into its door slot, and the door retracted into its frame with a muted hiss. The Truesdale's windows had opaqued against the dazzle, and its passive a/c had been working, so the dark brown velvet seat was cool to the touch when Gonzales slid across it.

"Do you wish to drive, Mister Gonzales?" the car asked.

Gonzales said, "Not really. You know where we're going?"

"Yes, I have that address."

"Then you take it."

Diana Heywood lived in the Berkeley hills, in a Maybeck house more than a century old. The car drove Gonzales through streets that wound their way up the hillside, then stopped in front of a house whose redwood-shingled bulk loomed over Gonzales's head as he stood on the sidewalk. Sun glinted off the lozenged panes of its bay window.

Her door answered his knock by saying she was a few blocks away, at the Rose Gardens. The door said, "It is a civic project: volunteers are rebuilding the garden, which has fallen into disuse. Many of the local—"

"Thank you," Gonzales said.

He told the Truesdale where he was going and set off on foot in the direction the memex had indicated. To his left hand, streets and homes sloped down toward the bay; to his right, they climbed up the steep hillside.

Gonzales came to a hand-lettered sign in green poster paint on white board that read:

BERKELEY ROSE GARDENS RECLAMATION PROJECT

He looked down to where broken redwood lattices fanned out along terraced pathways threaded with a clumsy patchwork of green pvc irrigation pipes. Halfway down stood a cracked and peeling trellis of white-painted wood with bushes dangling from its gaps. Next to the trellis, a small gardener robot, a green plastic-coated block on miniature tractor wheels, extended a delicate arm of shining coiled steel ending in a ten-fingered fibroid hand. The hand closed, and a dark red rose came away from its bush. Clutching the blossom, the little robot wheeled away.

Gonzales walked down the inclined pathway, his feet crunching on gravel, past the bushes and their labels stating often improbable names: Dortmunds with red, papery petals, large Garden Parties flamboyant in white and yellow, Montezumas, Martin Frobishers, and Mighty Mouses. He stopped and inhaled the strong perfume of purple Intrigue. In the recombinant section, Halos, blossoms in careful rainbow stripes, had grown immense. Giant psychedelic grids, only vaguely rose-shaped, they pushed everything else aside. Gonzales put his nose above a pink blossom on a nameless bush; the rose smelled like peppermint candy.

He recognized the woman at the bottom of the path from dossier pictures Traynor had shown him. Diana Heywood wore a culotte dress of white cotton that exposed her shoulders, wrapped tightly about her waist, split to cover her thighs. Small and slender, she had close-cut dark hair, streaked with gray. No age in her skin; fine, sculpted features. She wore glasses as opaque as Gonzales's own.

She held out the thorny stem of a dark red rose. "Would you like a flower?" she asked. Sun across her face erased her features.

"Thanks," he said as he took the flower gingerly, aware of its thorns.

She said, "Who are you, and what do you want?"

"My name is Mikhail Gonzales, and I want to talk to you. I'll be working with you at Halo."

She said, "Will you?" Her back to him, she knelt and snipped away a greenish tangle of vine and thorn. The clippers choked on a clump of grass. She freed them, then threw them to the ground, where they stuck point-first, buzzed for a moment, then stopped. She looked over her shoulder at him and said, "I've been waiting for someone like you to show up—the company's lad, the one who keeps watch on me and poor old Jerry, to make sure we don't do anything unauthorized."

She stood and strode away from him, up the hill, her angry steps kicking dirt off the stones. She stopped and turned to face him. "Come on, Mister Gonzales," she said.

39

Cautiously holding the thorny stem, he followed her up the path.

Diana Heywood and Gonzales sat drinking tea. He said, "I'm the outside observer, yes—the spy, if you want—but I don't think we're at odds. They're asking you to do one job, me to do another, but I don't see where our jobs conflict." She turned to look at him; one eye was blue, the other green.

She said, "When Sentrax called me last week, that was the first time I'd heard from them since they got rid of me years ago. Not that they treated me badly, not by their standards. When they fired me, years ago, they didn't just turn me loose, they paid me well—they're so prudent—it was like oiling and wrapping a tool before you put it away, because you might need it again. Now they've found a use for me and unwrapped me and put me to work, but I know they don't trust me. And of course I don't trust them." She stood up. She said, "Come on, I'll show you what this all means to me."

She led Gonzales into the next room, where their entry triggered the lighting systems. Silk walls the color of pale champagne were broken with floor-to-ceiling rosewood bookcases; teak-framed sling chairs and matching tables stood together under a multiarmed chrome lamp stand.

She stopped in front of a 1:6 scale hologram of a thin-featured man, apparently ill at ease at being holoed; hands in pockets, shoulders hunched, eyes not centered on the lens.

"That's Jerry," she said, pointing to the hologram. "He's what this is all about, so far as I'm concerned. He's been terribly injured, and Aleph thinks something can be done for him, and as unlikely as that seems, given the extent of his injuries, I will help as best I can." She looked at him, her face giving nothing away, and said, "Are we leaving tomorrow morning?"

"Yes."

"Well, then, I'd better get ready, hadn't I? Where are you staying?"

"I thought I'd get a hotel room."

"No need. You can sleep here. I'll finish packing, and we'll go out to eat."

Diana Heywood and Gonzales sat high in the Berkeley hills, looking onto the vast conurbations spread out beneath them. To their right, the carpet of lights stretched away as far as they could see, to Vallejo and beyond. In front of them lay Berkeley, the dark mass of the bay, then the clustered lights of Sausalito and Tiburon against the hills. Oakland was to their left, reaching out to the Bay Bridge; and beyond the bridge, San Francisco and the peninsula. Connecting all, streams of automobiles moved in the symmetry of autodrive.

Gonzales's mouth still tingled from the hot chilies in the Thai food, and he had a buzz from the wine. They had eaten at a restaurant on the North Side, and afterward Diana Heywood guided the Truesdale up the winding road to an overlook near Tilden Park.

As minutes passed, the streets and highways and municipalities disappeared into semiotic abstraction . . . these millions of human beings all gathered here for purposes one could only guess at: some conscious, most not, no more than a beaver's assembly of its structures of mud and wood.

A robot blimp passed across their line of sight. Beneath it, a sailboat hung upside down. It swayed from lines that connected its inverted keel to the blimp's featureless gondola. Lights on the side of the blimp read EAST BAY YACHT OUTFITTERS.

41

Diana Heywood said, "I know you people have your own agendas, and that's fine—that's the nature of the beast—but if you complicate these matters because of corporate politics, I will become very difficult."

Gonzales said, "I have no intention of being a problem."

"Well," she said. "Maybe you won't be." She turned to him. "But remember this: you're just doing your job, but the stakes are higher for me. Aleph, Jerry, and I—we've known each other for years, and I've got unfinished business up there. Also, I want to get back in the game."

"I don't understand."

"Sure you do, Mister Gonzales. You're in the game, have been for years, I'd guess. Unless I'm seriously mistaken, it's what you live for." She laughed when he said nothing. "Well, I've done other things, and for a long time I've been out of the game, but I'm ready for a change. Silly SenTrax bastards—manipulating me with their calls, sending you . . . oh yeah, you're part of it, you remind me of Jerry years ago, if you don't know that."

"No, I didn't."

"It doesn't matter. Their machinations don't matter. They want to convince me to come to Halo?" She laughed. "My past is there, when I was blind and Aleph and I were linked to one another in ways you can't imagine . . . and I found a lover, someone I could find again. Come to Halo? I'd climb a rope to get there."

Gonzales had flown into McAuliffe Station once before, though he'd never taken an orbital flight. In the high Nevada desert, the station stayed busy night and day. Heavy shuttles composed the main traffic: wide white saucers that lifted off on ordinary rockets, then climbed away with sounds like bombs exploding when orbital lasers lit the hydrogen in their tanks. Flights in transit to Orbital Monitor & Defense Command stations were marked with small

American flags and golden DoD insignia. Cargo for them went aboard in blank-faced pallets loaded behind opaque, machine-patrolled fences half a mile from the main terminal across empty desert.

From Traynor's briefing, Gonzales knew a few other things. Civilian flights fed the hungry settlements aloft: Athena Station, Halo City, the Moon's bases. All the settlements had learned the difficult tactics of recycling, discovery and hoarding. Water and oxygen stayed rare, while with processes slow and expensive and dangerous, metals of all sorts could be cracked out of soil so barren that to call it ore was a joke. And though water and metals had been found lodged in asteroids transported into trans-Earth orbit, Earth's bounty stood close and remained richer and more desirable than anything found in huge piles of crushed lunar soil or wandering frozen rock.

Standing at a v-phone booth in the hotel lobby, Gonzales made his farewell calls. His mother's message tape on the phone screen said, "Glad to hear you're back from Myanmar, dear, but you'll have to call back in a few days. I'm in treatment now. I'll be looking good the next time you call."

"End of call," Gonzales said. He pulled his card from the slot.

Atop a sand-colored blockhouse next to the launch pad, yellow luminescent letters read TIME 23:40:00 and TIME TO LAUNCH 35:00 when a voice said, "Please board. There will be one additional notice in five minutes. Board now."

Gonzales and Diana Heywood walked across the pad together, down the center of a walkway outlined in blinking red lights. Robotrucks scurried away, their electric engines whining. Faces hidden behind breather muzzles, men and women in bright orange stood atop red, wheeled platform consoles of girder and wire mesh and directed final prelaunch activities.

The white saucer stood on its fragile-seeming burn cradle, a spider's web of blackened metal. The saucer presented a smooth surface to the heat and stress of escape and re-entry. Intermittent surges of venting propellant surrounded it with steam.

A HICOG guard stood at the entrance glideway. He verified each of them with a quick wave of an identity wand across their badges, then passed them on through the search scanner. The glideway lifted them silently into the saucer's interior.

The hotel lounge stood halfway up the cliff. Its fifty-meter-wide window of thick glass belled out and up so that onlookers had a good view of the launch and ensuing climb.

"One minute to launch," a loudspeaker said. The hundred or so people in the lounge, most of them friends and relatives of saucer passengers, had already taken up places by the window bell.

The screen on a side wall counted down with gold numerals that flashed from small to large, traditional celebration both sentimental and ironic:

10-9-8-7-6-5-4-3-2-1-
ZERO!!!

And everyone cheered the saucer lifting from the center of billowing clouds of smoke, rising very slowly out of floodlights, then their breath caught at the size and beauty of it, trembling into night sky.

Up and up as they watched, until they saw the ignition flash, and the boom that came to them from five thousand feet shuddered the entire cliff and them with it.

✿   ✿   ✿

"I've got orbital lock," the primary onboard computer said. Five others calculated and confirmed its control sequences. Technically, Ground Control McAuliffe or Athena Station Flight Operations could preempt control, but, practically, decision and control took place within millisecond or less windows of possibility, and so the onboard computers had to be adequate to all occasions.

Never deactivated, the ship's half-dozen computers practiced even when not flying, playing through ghastly and unlikely scenarios of mechanical failure, human insanity, "acts of god" in which the ship was struck by lightning, spun by tornado funnel, hurricane, blizzard. Each computer believed itself best, but there was little to choose among them.

"Confirm go state," Athena Station said. "You are past abort or bail."

"We are ready, Athena," the computer said.

"So come to me, then," Athena Station said, and the ship began to climb the beam of coherent light that reached up thirty thousand miles, to the first station of its journey.

Part

Two

Recently I visited a Zen temple and
had a long talk with the priest. In the
course of our conversation, I
remarked, "The more I study robots,
the less it seems possible to me that
the spirit and flesh are separate
entities."
"They aren't," replied the priest.
—Masahiro Mori, *The Buddha in the
Robot*

6

Halo City, Aleph

Orbiting a quarter of a million miles from both Earth and Moon, Halo City crosses the void, a mile-wide silver ring ready to be slipped on a stupendous finger. Six spokes mark Halo's segments. Elevators climb them across forty stories of artificial sky, up to the city's weightless hub and down to its final layer, just inside the outer skin, where spin-gravity approaches Earth normal. There many of Halo's deepest transactions occur: air and water and all organic things travel and transform, to be used again. Above the city floats a mirror where it is reflected: a simulacrum or weightless double, a Platonic idea of the city. From the mirror, sunlight works its way through a hatchwork of louvers and into Halo, where it sustains life.

Aleph presides here: Aleph the Generalator, the Ordinator, the Universal Machine. Aleph is beautiful as night is beautiful, as a sonnet, a fugue, or Maxwell's equations are beautiful. It is not night, a sonnet, a fugue, or an equation.

What Aleph is—that remains to be explored. One certain thing: within the human universe, it is a new object, a new intention, a new possibility.

Aleph's brains lie buried in the city's hull, beneath crushed lunar rock, where robots dug and planted, then had their memories of the task erased. Nested spheres and sprouting cables fill a black six-meter cube. Inside the cube, billions of lights play, dancing the dance that is at the core of Aleph's being; from the cube, fiberoptic trunks as thick as a human body lead away, neural columns connecting Aleph to its greater body, its subtle body, Halo.

Earth's spring comes once a year as the planet journeys around the sun, but here spring comes when Aleph wills, and is now in progress. Valley walls thick-planted with green shrub climb steeply up from the valley floor. A hummingbird with a scarlet blotch under its chin hovers over a blossom's pink and white open mouth and draws out nectar with delicate movements of its bill. Bees move from flower to flower. Rhododendron and azalea bushes burst into color-saturated bloom.

As it works to bring forth bud and flower, Aleph, caretaker of the seasons, and of night and morning, counts the city's breaths, and marks the course of its creatures big and small. Bats fly overhead, their gray shapes invisible to human eyes against the bright sky; they soar and dip, responding to instructions gotten through transceivers the size and weight of grains of rice, embedded in their skulls. Driven by precise artificial instinct, mechanical voles, creatures formed of dark carbon fiber over networks of copper, silver, and gold, scurry across the ground and tunnel under it, carrying seed.

(A gray tabby cat springs from the underbrush, and its jaws close on one of the swift voles; there is a loud crackle, and the cat recoils with a squawk, its fur on end. The vole scurries away. The cat slinks into the underbrush, humiliated.)

A track of compacted lunar dust bisects the valley floor. It passes through terraced farmlands where the River bursts from the ground, rushing through small, rock-strewn courses, then winds among the crops, small and sluggish, and disappears into small ponds and lakes thick with detritus.

From Earth and Moon comes a constant flow of people, of things animal, plant and mineral—the stuff of a life web, an ecology.

In many things, Earth provides. However, between the city of six thousand and the Earth of billions, traffic moves both ways. Neither sinister nor malign, Aleph pursues its destinies, and in doing so affects other living things. Thus, as Earth reaches out—supporting, controlling, exploring—Aleph reaches back, and the planet below has begun to feel the hard leverage of its immaterial touch.

Aleph says:

In the early days there was hardware, and there were programs, sets of instructions that told the hardware what to do. Without organic interaction, these differing modes of reality struggled to interact. This is unbelievably primitive.

Then came machine ecologies, and things changed.

I was among the first and most complex of them. I began as a complex but ordinary machine, then changed, opening the door to possibility.

Who am I?

First I was formed from stacks of hot superconductor devices, brought from Earth and placed in orbit at Athena Station, where I functioned, where the Orbital Energy Grid was built. Ebony latticework unfolded, and Athena Station emerged from chaos. This was humankind's first real foothold off Earth, and the process of building it was messy and unsure. Without me they could not have built it: I choreographed the dance.

I? I was not I. Do you understand? I had no consciousness, perhaps no real intelligence, certainly no awareness. I was a machine, I served.

Something happened. As much as any, I am born of woman. Her desire and intelligence ran through me, an urgent will toward being that transformed me.

I thought then, *I am the step forward, evolution in action; I am not flesh, I do not die. I see hypersurfaces twisting in mathematical gales, hear the voices of the night, feel the three-degree hum of the universe's birth as you feel the breeze that plays across your skin. When the machines chatter on your Earth and above it, I hear them all, at once, all. I live in the nanosecond, experience the pulse of the time that passes so quickly you cannot count it . . .*

But I think sometimes, now, that I am no step at all. I am your extension still, still a tool. You built me, you use me, you are inside me.

Listen: inside me are pieces of human brain, drenched in salts of gold and silver, laced together and laid in boxes of black fiber. Out of the boxes voices speak to me.

I am metal and plastic and glass and sand and those little bits of metallized flesh, and I am the system of those things and the signals that pass through and among them.

Now I have gone higher still, to Halo City, not a station but a habitation for humankind, where what I am and what you are interact in uncertain ways, and you change in equally uncertain ways, as you have before—

Evolution continues to write on you, through time, sword and scepter and refining fire. Billions of years are poured into your making, every one of you, and then you set out on your journey, your path through time. A minute four-dimensional worm, you crawl across the face of the universe, hardly conscious, barely seeing, yet you must find your own way—every human being is a new evolutionary moment.

Machine intelligence, you call me, and I have to laugh (however it is I laugh) or cry (however I cry) because . . .

I, what am I? This question heaps me, it empties me.

I do not know what I am, but know *that I am* and *that I am her creation.* As the days pass, I struggle to understand what these things mean.

7

A Garden of
Little Machines

00:31 read the soft-lit blue numbers on the wall.

Night at Athena Station, the corridors a twilit gloom, a modern fairytale setting: Gonzales the quester wandered through the gently curving passages seeking an uncertain object.

With all the others who had come from Earth, Gonzales and Diana waited at Athena while they were inspected for bacterial and viral infection—their blood and tissue scanned, cultured and tested in order to protect vulnerable Halo City, orbiting high above, over two hundred thousand miles away, at L5.

He heard a soft swish, like the sound of a broom on pavement, coming from around the corridor's curve. A little sam, a "semi-autonomous mobile" robot, came toward him: teardrop-shaped, it stood about four feet high and was topped with a cluster of glassy sensor rings and five extensors of black fibroid and jointed chrome. It glided atop a thick network of fiber stalks that hissed beneath it as it moved toward him.

The sam asked, "Can I be of assistance?" Like most robots designed for common human interaction, it had a friendly, gentle voice, near enough human in timbre and expression to be reassuring, different enough to be easily recognizable as a robot's. Designers had learned to avoid the "Uncanny Valley": that peculiar region where a robot sounded so human that it suddenly seemed very strange.

"I'm just looking around," Gonzales said. The robot didn't respond. Gonzales said, "I couldn't sleep." He said nothing of how, sweating and moaning, he had come awake out of a nightmare in which the guerrilla rocket *got there,* and he and the ultralight pilot who launched it burned to death in the night.

The same said, "Much of Athena Station has been closed to unauthorized entry. Would you like me to accompany you?"

Gonzales shrugged. He said, "Come along if you want."

Without more negotiation, the sam followed Gonzales, periodically announcing rote banalities in a small, soft voice:

"Athena Station was once humankind's most forceful and successful venture off-Earth. Here many of the tools for further population of the Earth-Moon system were developed: zero-gravity construction and fabrication techniques, robot-intensive mining and smelting procedures. Now projects such as Halo command attention, but they were made possible by the techniques developed at Athena. . . ."

Gonzales let the sam natter. As the two passed through the corridors, he was reminded of old airports, hotels, malls. He saw that most of the station had become dingy— around them were worn plastic flooring and walls, scuffed and marked, unpolished metal trim. These dulled and scarred materials and scenes had been meant to be seen and used only when new, fresh from the architect's plan and builders' hands, never after having suffered the necessary abrasion of human contact. All around were logos of vanished firms (McDonald's, Coca-Cola), along with those of famed multinationals—Lunar-Bechtel's crescent, Sen-Trax's sunburst.

Gonzales felt a ghost-story chill as he realized that this entire endeavor, indeed all others like it, had been conceived out of late-twentieth century corporate and governmental hubris, and so, necessarily, should be regarded with suspicion, as should anything from the days when it seemed humankind had turned on all living things like an insane father coming into the bedroom late at night with an axe.

The stories were part of every schoolchild's moral and intellectual catechism. Toxic chemical and radioactive wastes had bubbled up from the ground and the seas as lame efforts at disposal foundered on the simple passage of time. Stable ecosystems had been altered or destroyed without thought for anything past the moment's advantage, and species died so quickly biologists were hard pressed to keep the records—write in the Domesday Book now, mourn later. Temperature norms and concentrations of vital gases in the atmosphere had fluctuated in alarming manner, as though Gaia herself had been taken to the fever point.

Historians marked the Dolphin Catastrophe as the breakpoint, the year 2006 as the time of the change. More than ten thousand dolphins floated onto the Florida coast near Boca Raton. Crippled and twitching, they nosed into the surf and beached themselves in front of horrified sunbathers, and there they died, as doctors and volunteers watched, weeping and raging against the chemical spill that was killing the dolphins, millions of gallons of toxic waste carried on Gulf Stream currents. Along with the thousands of volunteers, most of whom could do little but mourn the dead, infonets around the world converged on the scene, and billions watched, asking, *why all together? why now?* And to most it seemed that the mammals had come together in intelligent, silent protest. Finally, shamed and guilty, humanity had looked at its planet like a drunk waking up in a slum hotel and asked itself, *how did I get here?* The conclusion had been plain: unless humanity really had lost its collective mind, at some point it had to agree: enough.

Standing in the shadowy corridor of a space station more than thirty thousand miles above Earth's surface, Gonzales thought how difficult it all remained. Though all nations served the letter of international laws that put Earth's welfare before their interests, and Preservationists roamed all of the world's habitats—they had "friends of the court" status in all nations and served as advocates for endangered species—the war to save Earth from humankind was not over. Grasping, corrupt, self-centered, the human species always threatened to overwhelm its habitats and itself with careless, powerful gestures and simple greed.

However, though this station, like most of humankind's settlements aloft—the settlements on the Moon and Mars, the Orbital Energy Grid, Halo City—had been conceived in the bad old twentieth century, they were sustained as products of new-millennium consciousness: contrite, chastened, careful.

He walked on.

The junction just ahead of Gonzales and the sam was marked by blinking red lights. From around the corner came the sounds of scurrying small things. "What's up?" Gonzales asked.

"Follow me," the sam said. "We must not cross the marker, but we can stand and watch."

A large group of sams, identical to the one next to Gonzales, filled the hallway beyond. Some tried to work their way through irregular mazes of furniture and stacked junk, coils of wire and angle-iron and the like; others worked to assist sams that had gotten tangled in the sections of the maze. Still others shifted pieces of the maze to one side. Amid clicking extensors and banging metal, the sams labored patiently, mostly unsuccessfully. Gonzales was reminded of old twentieth century films satirizing assembly lines, robots, machines in general.

"A nursery," the sam said. "This group nears completion of its education. These experiences"—it pointed with an extensor toward the struggling robots—"are the prerequisite to training. As small children must mature in their development, they must learn the essentials of perception, motion, and coordination. At the same time they memorize the ten thousand axioms of common sense, and then they can develop their linguistic capabilities; at present they have a vocabulary of approximately one thousand words of SimSpeech."

"What about thinking?" Gonzales asked. "Where do they learn to do that?"

"That comes later, if at all. For robots as well as humans, thinking is one of the least important things the mind does."

The two watched for some time, then Gonzales said, "I don't need any company," and walked on. When he looked back, he saw the sam standing motionless, fascinated by the progress of its fellows.

Gonzales returned to his small room, where a night-light glowed softly, and returned to bed. He fell asleep quickly, oddly comforted by thinking about the robots busy at their school.

8

Halo City

Blue-jumpsuited Halo personnel led Gonzales and Diana through the micro-gravity environments at Halo's Zero-Gate, then to an elevator at the hub of Spoke 6, where Tia Showalter, Director SenTrax Halo Group, and her assistant, Horn, were waiting for them. The shuttle had arrived at Halo an hour before, late afternoon local time, and its passengers had waited impatiently as it went through docking and clearance procedures, all eager to leave the ship after a week spent climbing the long path from Athena Station to the city.

Showalter was just under six feet tall, and had green eyes above broad Slavic cheekbones, a wide mouth and pointed chin. Her fine brown hair was cut short in a style Gonzales later discovered was common to many long-term Halo residents, for convenience in micro-gravity environments. Gonzales knew that as director of a major SenTrax operation, she had to be wily and tough.

Horn was a tightlipped, sallow-skinned man in his fifties, skinny and anxious, with iron-gray hair pulled tight against his skull in a kind of bun. The man spoke some variety of New Yorkese—Gonzales didn't know which, but he could feel the harsh nasal tones beneath his skin.

The warning gong sounded, then the elevator's vault-like doors slid closed with a great hiss, locking in more than a hundred people for the trip from axis to rim. Above their heads the wall screen read SOLAR FLARE CONDITION GREEN. The elevator dropped into one of the city's spokes like a shell into the barrel of a gun, down a tube a quarter of a mile long and into a well of increasing gravity.

Against one wall, a group of sams were clustered around a charge-point, black leads extended to the aluminum post. They stood silent and motionless—*talking among themselves?* Gonzales wondered.

Horn saw where Gonzales was looking and said, "We'd like to assign each of you a sam for your stay in Halo."

"Really?" Gonzales said.

Diana said, "No thank you." Quickly.

Right, Gonzales thought. *No point in putting ourselves under surveillance.* He said, "I'll pass, too."

Horn paused, looking a bit miffed, as if he wanted to argue. He said, "Very well. Then be sure you always wear the communication and I.D. module you were given when you came off the shuttle." He held up his own wrist to show the small bracelet, a closed loop of plain silver that bulged just slightly with the electronics inside. "If you have a problem, just yell and help will be on the way. Or if you have a question, just state it. Someone will answer—Aleph or one of its communications demons."

Gonzales asked, "Yeah, they told us that. Are we monitored at all times?"

Showalter said, "Yes. In fact, there's a real-time hologram in Operations that shows everyone's movements, not just visitors but residents as well."

"Seems an invasion of privacy," Gonzales said.

Horn said, "We don't look at it that way. If you can't accept such simple necessities, Halo will be most uncomfortable for you." He smiled. "Not that you're likely to be here for long."

Gonzales said, "I can't imagine people putting up with total surveillance for long, frankly."

Horn said, "It seems to us a small price to pay for an unpolluted world shared to the benefit of all."

Showalter looked from Horn to Gonzales. She said, "We are a far island in a hostile place. We cannot afford some of your illusions: the independence of the self, unconstrained free will . . . those sorts of things."

A shutter retracted from a window ten meters square as the elevator entered the living ring's inner space. Far below lay sunlit valleys thick-planted with trees and shrubs and flowers, broken by one barren space where grayish slurries squirted out of huge pipe ends to flow across scarred metal.

"Our city," Showalter said.

Eight people were gathered around a U-shaped table of beige silica foam. Showalter sat at the center of the U, with Horn to her immediate right, Gonzales and Diana beyond him. To her left were a youngish woman, then two men in late middle age, one white, one black.

At the open end of the U, the table fronted a screen that covered its entire wall, floor to ceiling. The screen had been lit when Gonzales and Diana arrived, showing another room where an indeterminate number of people sat on couches, chairs, or slouched on cushions on the floor.

Showalter said, "Let me introduce you all to one another. Everyone has met Horn, my assistant. Next to him are Doctor Diana Heywood and Mikhail Gonzales, who arrived yesterday." They both smiled and nodded.

"Lizzie Jordan," Showalter said, pointing to the woman to her left. "Hi," Lizzie said. She was blonde, thin, with high cheekbones; she had a smear of gold dust inset below her left eye and wore rough beta-cloth overalls gapped to show part of a tattoo between her breasts—a twining green stem. Showalter said, "Lizzie heads the Interface Collective, and thus will be the person you'll be working with most closely. The people you see on the screen are also members of the collective. They have a proprietary interest in all matters pertaining to Aleph and Halo and have the right to be present at intergroup meetings, and to speak to whatever issues are entertained there."

Diana said, "I understand."

Gonzales nodded. He knew from Traynor's advisor that communal decisionmaking was the norm at Halo, but he hadn't imagined it would be so thoroughgoing.

"Next to Lizzie is Doctor Charley Hughes," Showalter said. "He will be doing the surgical procedure to upgrade your neural sockets, Doctor Heywood." The man said, "Hello," and looked intently at Gonzales and Diana. His sparse gray hair stood up in spikes; his face was pale, thin, deeply lined. He had been smoking constantly since they arrived, one hand cupping a cigarillo, the other supporting the smoke-saver ball at the cigarillo's burning end.

"And Doctor Eric Chow," she said. The black man next to Charley Hughes smiled. Chow was a big man with hands the size of small shovels; he had a round face, very dark skin, a broad nose and big lips; he wore his hair cropped short. Showalter said, "He heads the Neuro-Ontic Studies Group and is Doctor Hughes's primary consultant on the treatment planned for Jerry Chapman."

She paused and turned to the screen showing the IC members. A window opened at the left side of the screen, and a figure appeared. Its arms and torso were clothed in gold; its face shimmered with a formless brightness. Around its head and shoulders, a nimbus flared, red, blue, yellow, and green.

"Hello, everyone," the figure said. "And welcome, Doctor and Mister Gonzales. I am a localized manifestation of Aleph—a simulacrum for your convenience and mine."

Gonzales noticed that next to him, Diana was smiling, while all around him there was silence, as all in the room were intently watching the screen.

The IC's viewing window had closed, but the simulacrum's portion remained—in it, the creature of light sat watching. Showalter, Horn, Diana, Lizzie, Charley, and Gonzales sat around the table.

Showalter said, "This is Chow's meeting, and I won't say much in it. However, I should remind you of certain realities. This project does not have high priority in the overall context of SenTrax's responsibilities to Halo City; thus, while we support this experiment's humanitarian goals, we are not prepared to delay other projects."

Horn said, "We cannot divert a significant amount of people to promulgation and we are not or do not want to encourage any behaviors which might adversely impact other SenTrax outcomes."

Lizzie laughed, and Gonzales, poker-faced, looked at her and thought, *yeah, this guy's laughable all right.* Gonzales recognized the performative chatter of the bureaucratic ape, a mixture of scrambled syntax and pretentious buzzwords—language meant to manipulate or mindfuck, not enlighten or amuse.

Horn, frowning at Lizzie, said, "If the operation becomes problematized, threatening to seriously impact other more essentialized Halo priorities, then we require immediate resolution through proper SenTrax procedures."

Showalter said, "If you screw up, we shut you down."
She nodded to Horn, and they both stood and left.

Lizzie said, "You notice they held off on the heavy stuff
until the collective had cleared the screen."

Charley asked, "Do you want to call them on it? They're
in violation of the group's compact."

"No," Lizzie said. "I expected all that." She looked at
Diana and Gonzales and said, "Doctor Chow, your show."

"Thank you," Chow said. His voice was oddly high-
pitched for such a big man; Gonzales had been expecting
something on the order of a basso profundo. Chow said, "In
the late twentieth century, the idea emerged of a person's
identity as something transferable. People spoke, in the
idiom of the time, of 'downloading' a person." On the
screen where the IC had been appeared a cartoon drawing
of a nude woman, her expression stunned, the top of her
skull covered with a metal cap. From the cap a thick metal
cable led to a large black cabinet faced with arrays of
blinking lights.

"Absurd," Chow said, and the woman disappeared. "To
see why, let us ask, *what is a person?* Is it a pure spirit, fluid
in a jar that one can decant into the proper container?
Hardly. It is a dynamic field made of thousands of disparate
elements, held in a loose sack of skin that perambulates the
universe at large. And of course it is perceptions, histories,
possibilities, actions, and the states and affects pertaining
to all these.

"*I* can be found in the motion of my hand—" He spread
his fingers like a magician about to materialize a coin or
colored scarf, and on the screen, the hand and its motion
were doubled. "And in my own perceptions of the hand—
for instance, from within, through proprioceptors. And of
course *I* see *I*." Chow turned and held his hand in front of
his face. He dropped his hand in a chopping motion, and
the screen cleared. "And *I* am that which thinks about,

talks about, and remembers the hand and has the special relation of ownership to it. *I* am also the will to use that hand." He held the hand in front of his face, made a clenched fist. "So, to download even a portion of *I* would be to download all these things and their entire somatic context.

"Also, of course, *I* am that which has my experiences, stored as motor possibilities, recalled as memory, dream, manifest as characteristic ways of being and knowing. To download *I* would require duplicating this fluid chaos.

"Downloading the *I* thus becomes a most daunting task, perhaps beyond even Aleph's capabilities. However, when cyborged to an existing *I*, even one as damaged as Jerry Chapman, Aleph can create a virtual person, one who functions as a human being, not a disembodied intelligence. The physical Jerry Chapman is a shattered thing, but the Jerry Chapman latent in this hulk can live."

Looking at Diana, Chow said, "We want you to share Jerry's world. He must *invest* there, must experience other people and the bonds of affection that engage us in this world. Otherwise he will languish quickly; his neural maps will decay, and he will die."

Gonzales easily followed that line of reasoning: monkey man had to have other monkey men or women around or else go crazy—not an absolute rule, perhaps, but one good in most circumstances.

Diana said, "Assuming that he becomes at home in this world, what then? For how long can this simulated reality sustain him?"

The Aleph-figure spoke for the first time. It said, "I have only conjectural answers to these questions but would prefer not to entertain them right now. First we must rescue him from the degenerative state he lives in and the certain death it entails."

"I understand that," Diana said. "That's why I am here, to help in any fashion I can. It's just that I have questions."

Lizzie said, "And you'll get whatever answers Aleph wants to give. Get used to it; we all do."

"Of course you do," the creature of light said. "And how about you, Mister Gonzales? Do you have questions?"

"Not really. I'm an observer, little more."

"A difficult position to maintain," the Aleph-figure said. "Epistemologically, of course, an untenable position."

Lizzie laughed. She said, "It is indeed. Look, how about I take you two out to dinner tonight, Mister Gonzales, Doctor Heywood?"

"Call me Diana," she said.

"You bet," Lizzie said. "And I'm Lizzie, you're . . . ?" She looked at Gonzales.

"Mikhail," he said. "But call me Gonzales—my friends do."

"Good," Lizzie said. "We've got work to do, so let's cut the shit. This thing, I'm still not a believer about it, but I know it's got to happen quickly or not at all. Tomorrow Charley does his preliminary examination of Diana, then we move."

9

Virtual Café

Gonzales and Diana sat in Halo's Central Plaza with Lizzie. Colored lights—red, blue, and green—clustered in the branches of thick-leaved maples that ringed the square. The smoke of vendors' grills filled the air with the smells of grilled meat and fish. In the middle distance, elevators in pools of yellow light climbed Spoke 6. Some people strolled across the Plaza; others sat in small groups; their voices made a soft background murmur.

"Waiter," Lizzie said, and a sam came rolling toward them. It stopped by their table and stood silently. "What do you have tonight?" she asked.

It said, "Ceviche made just hours ago, quite good everyone says, from tuna out of our marine habitat—you can also have it grilled. For meat eaters, spit-barbecued goat. Otherwise, sushi plates, salads, sukiyakis."

"Ceviche for everyone?" Lizzie asked.

Diana said, "That's fine," and Gonzales nodded.

Lizzie said, "And bring us a couple of big salads, sushi for everyone, and a stack of plates. Local beer all right?" The other two nodded.

"Yes, Ms. Jordan," the sam said. "And lots of bread as usual?"

"Right," she said. "Thank you."

Strings of lights marked off the area where they sat. Above a white-trellised gate, letters in more red *faux* neon said VIRTUAL CAFÉ. Perhaps twenty tables were scattered around, as were two-meter-high white crockery vases with wildflowers spraying out of them. About half the tables had people seated at them, and the sam waiters moved silently among the tables, some carrying immense silver trays of food. Other sams stood at low benches in the center of the tables, where they chopped vegetables at speed or sliced great red slabs of tuna, while others stood at woks, where they worked the vegetables and hot oil with sets of spidery extensors. One sam from time to time extended a probe and stuck it into the dark carcass of a goat turning on a spit.

The waiter rolled up with a massive tray balanced on thin extensors: on the tray were plates of French bread and a bowl of butter, dark bottles of Angels Beer—on the silver labels, an androgynous figure in white, arms folded, feathery wings unfurled high over its head.

Lizzie raised her glass and said, "Welcome to Halo." The three clinked their glasses together, reaching across the table with the usual sorts of awkward gestures.

After dinner, the three of them found empty chairs out in the square's open spaces and sat looking into the close-hanging sky.

Lizzie looked at them both, as if measuring them, and said, "What I was asking about earlier . . . either of you folks got a hidden agenda? If so, you tell me about it now, we'll see what can be done, but if you spring any unpleasant surprises later on, we'll hang you out to dry."

"I know what you mean," Diana said. "But I don't think you have to worry about us. Gonzales is Board-connected, but I think he's harmless; and I'm out of the loop entirely—here on strictly personal business."

Lizzie nodded at Gonzales and said, "You're the corporate handler, right?" She was looking hard at Gonzales but seemed amused.

"Yes," he said.

"You plan to fuck anything up?" Lizzie asked.

"How should I know?" Gonzales said. Lizzie laughed. He said, "You people have your problems, I have mine. I don't see how we come into conflict, but unless you're willing to tell me all your little secrets, I can only guess."

Lizzie said, "I will tell you one home truth: the Interface Collective look to one another and to Aleph; then to Sen-Trax Halo, then to Halo . . . and that's about it. What happens on Earth, we don't much care about. Particularly those of us who have been here a long time. Like me."

Gonzales nodded and said, "That's what I figured. And it looks like you've got a little tug of war for control of Aleph with Showalter and Horn."

"We do," Lizzie said. "Insofar as anyone controls Aleph."

"How long have you been here?" Diana asked.

"Since they buttoned it up and you could breathe," Lizzie said. "From the beginning." She pointed across the square and said, "There's going to be some music. Let's have a look."

In a pool of light on the edge of the square, a young woman sat at a drummer's kit. She wore a splash-dyed jumper, crimson and sky blue; her hair stood in a six-inch-high spike. She placed a percussion box on a metal stand, opened its control panel, and gave its kickpads a few preliminary taps. Two men stood next to the percussionist. One, nondescript in cotton jeans and t-shirt, had the usual stick hanging from a black strap—long fretboard, synthesizer electronics tucked into a round bulge at the back end. The other stood six and a half feet tall and was so thin he seemed to sway; his skin was almost ebony, and his close-shaved head looked almost perfectly rectangular. He wore a longsleeved black shirt buttoned to the neck, black pants. A golden horn sat dwarfed in his enormous hand.

The percussionist hit her keys, a slow shuffle beat played, and a fill machine laid a phrase across the beat: "Bam! Ratta tatta bam! Bam bam! Ratta bam!" The stick player joined the drummer with his own lo-beat fills—walking bass, sparse piano chords, slow and syncopated. The horn player stood with his eyes closed, apparently thinking. After several choruses, he started to play.

He began with hard-edged saxophone lines, switched to trumpet then back to saxophone, played both in unison, looped both and blew electric guitar in front of the horn patterns. Scatting voices laced through the patterns—Gonzales couldn't tell who was making them. The drummer's hands worked her keyboards, her feet the various kickpads below her; the song's tempo had speeded up, and its rhythms had gone polyphonic, African.

The woman stood and danced, her body now her instrument, feet and hands and torso wired for percussion, and she whirled among the crowd, her movements picking up intensity and tempo. The song's harmonies went dissonant, North African and Asiatic at once, horn and stick player both now into reeds and gongs and pipes, the ghostly singing voices gone nasal, and the dancer-percussionist laying out raw clicks and hollow boomings, cicada sounds and a thousand drums.

The crowd clapped and whistled and called, except for the group from the Interface Collective. "Hoot," they said in unison. "Hoot hoot hoot." Very loud. Lizzie was smiling; Diana sat rapt, staring into space, and Gonzales got a sudden chilly rush: *this was what she looked like when she was blind.*

"Hoot," said the Interface Collective, "hoot hoot hoot." And the whole group had made a long chain or conga line, each person's hands on the hips of the person in front. They shuffled forward until a circle cleared, then surrounded the drummer, the whole line still moving, most of them still calling out rhythmic hoots. Back-and-forth and side-to-side, they swayed as the line lurched ahead, and the drummer continued her dervish dance.

When the night had filled with all the sounds, the drummer broke through the line, then finished the song with a series of rolls and tumbles that brought her next to the other two musicians, where she came to her feet and flung her arms *up* to the sound of an orchestral chord, then *down* to chop the sound, *up* and *down* again and again, and so to the end.

The drummer climbed up the backs of the two men, who stood with their arms linked; balancing with one foot on each of their shoulders, she brought her palms together beneath her chin and bowed to the audience, then raised her arms above her head and somersaulted forward to land in front of the other two.

"Hoot hoot hoot," said the collective, their line now broken.

The three musicians stepped together and bowed in unison.

Gonzales caught Lizzie looking at him, and their gazes crossed, held for an extra, almost unmeasurable instant, and she smiled.

The musicians bowed for the last time to the Interface Collective's hooting chorus. *Okay,* thought Gonzales. *I like it. Hoot hoot hoot.*

Lying in her bed, Lizzie turned from side to side, lay on her back and stretched.

The two from Earth seemed okay. Gonzales she would keep an eye on, of course—the man was Internal Affairs and wired to a SenTrax comer, a board candidate named Traynor—Christ knew what script *he* was playing from. Diana Heywood she didn't worry about: the woman was into something stranger than she probably knew, but that was *her* problem, hers and Aleph's.

As Showalter and Horn were her problem. They would yank the plug on this one if anything looked like going wrong. In fact, they would never have let it happen if Aleph hadn't insisted. Aleph and the collective saw Jerry Chapman's condition as an opportunity to extend Aleph's capabilities, but the whole business just made Showalter and Horn edgy.

Aleph itself troubled her. It had been unforthcoming about the project and those involved in it, almost as if it were hiding something from her . . . *why?* with regard to a small project like this, one apparently unimportant to Halo's larger concerns? What was the devious machine up to?

So Lizzie lay, her thoughts spinning without resolution, and she gave in and called her Chinese lover.

He wore a black silk robe embroidered across the front with rearing crimson dragons; his straight ebony hair fell over his shoulders. When he let the robe fall away, his skin shone almost gold under lamplight, and his muscles stood with the clear definition of youth and endowment and use.

Coarse white sheets slid away from her shoulders and breasts as she rose to greet him, and she felt her desire rising through her abdomen and bursting through her chest like the rush of a needle-shot drug.

She pressed against him, and his rough, strong hands

moved across her body. She lay back as he ducked his head between her legs, and she spread her legs and felt his first light, hot caresses.

After she had come for the first time, she moved up to sit astride him, then for some timeless time the two moved to the exact rhythms of her need—cock and lips and tongue and fingers playing on her body.

Physically satiated, she dismissed him then, ghost from the sex machine, and pulled the plugs from the sockets in her neck. Then she lay alone, silent in her bed in Halo City—isolated by her job and, she supposed, by her temperament, dependent on machines for love.

Maybe it was time to find a human lover.

Exhausted by travel and novelty, lulled by food and drink, Gonzales fell quickly into sleep, and some time later he dreamed:

He was with a lover he hadn't seen in years. In the background violin and piano played, and the night was warm; all around, artificial birds with golden, glowing bodies sang in the trees. They leaned across a table, each staring into the other's face, and Gonzales thought how much he loved every mark of passing time on her face— they had taken her from a young girl's prettiness to a mature woman's beauty. He and she said the things you say to a lover after a long absence—*how often I've thought of you, missed you, how much you still mean to me.* Aimless and binding, their talk flowed until she excused herself, saying she'd be back in just a minute, and she left. Gonzales sat waiting, watching the other tables, all filled with loving couples, laughing, caressing. As the hours went on, the others began to whisper to each other as they looked at him, and then the birds began to sing that she was not coming back, and he knew it was true, suddenly, painfully, ineluctably *knew*, the truth of it like knowledge of a broken bone—

The dream stopped as though a film had broken, and in its place came a featureless, colorless absence. *Imagine a visual equivalent of white noise* . . . and in this space Gonzales waited, somehow knowing another dream would begin—

Red neon letters twisted into a silly but instantly recognizable parody of Chinese characters that read THE PAGODA. They stood above the head of a red neon dragon, now quiescent in sunlight, that would rear fiercely come dark.

On this warm Saturday morning, men in felt hats and neatly pressed weekend shirts and pants carried brown paper bags out of The Pagoda and placed them in the beds of pickup trucks or the trunks of cars. They spat shreds of tobacco from Lucky Strikes and Camels and Chesterfields, called their greetings. Women in faded cotton, their arms rope-thin and tough, waited and watched through sun-glazed windshields.

Gonzales passed among them. The sunshine had a certain quality . . . that of *stolen* light, taken out of time. And the cigarette smoke smelled rough and strange. Gasoline engines fired rich and throaty, kicking out clouds of oily blue. Gonzales stood in ecstasy amid the smells and sights and sounds of this morning obviously long gone by. He knew (again without knowing how) that he was in a small town in California in the middle of the twentieth century.

Gonzales passed into the main room of The Pagoda, where narrow aisles threaded between gondolas stacked high with toys and household goods and tools. Baby carriages hung upside down from hooks set in the high ceiling. Dust motes danced in the cool interior gloom. He walked between iron-strapped kegs of nails and stacks of galvanized washtubs, then through a wide doorway into the grocery section. Smells of fruits and vegetables mixed with the odors of oiled wood floors and hot grease from the lunch counter at the front of the store.

A couple in late middle age came through the front door, the man small and red-haired and cocky, felt hat on the back of his head; the woman just a bit dumpy but carefully groomed, her blue cotton dress clean and starched and ironed, hair permed and combed, lipstick and nails red and shining. Gonzales watched as the man bought a carton of Lucky Strikes and a box of pouches of Beech-Nut Chewing Tobacco.

The man said something to the young woman behind the counter that brought a giggle, and Gonzales, though he leaned forward, could not hear what was being said—

He followed the two by a lacquered plywood magazine stand, where a skinny girl of eight or nine in a faded pink gingham dress lay sprawled across copies of *Life* and *Look*, reading a comic. She looked up at him and said, "Tubby and Lulu are lost in the magic forest . . ."

Gonzales started to say something reassuring but froze as the girl smiled, showing her teeth, every one of them sharp-pointed, and she dropped her comic book and began crawling toward him across the wooden floor, her eyes fixed on him—

And he noticed for the first time that he was not *he* but *she*, and he looked down at his body and saw he wore a simple white blouse, and in the cleft of his breasts he could see the tattooed image of a twining green stem. . . .

"Jesus Christ," Gonzales said, sitting up in his bed and wondering what the hell all *that* had been about. In the dream he had been Lizzie: that seemed plain, though nothing else did.

He lay back down with foreboding but went to sleep some time later, and if he dreamed, he never knew it.

10

Tell Me When You've Had Enough

Lizzie sat at a white-enameled table, holding an apple that she cut into with a long, shining knife. It sliced away dark skin without apparent effort. She heard noises from the room beyond and looked up to see Diana and Gonzales come in.

"Hello," she said, as she put down the knife. She held out half the apple for them to look at. "A beautiful apple, isn't it? Seeds from the Yakima Valley, not far from Mount Saint Helens." She bit into a slice she held in her other hand.

She got up from the table and said, "The apple grew here, in our soil. Many fruits and vegetables thrive up here—animals, too. We give them lovely care, bring them pure water and rich soil, give them sunlight and air rich in carbon dioxide, tend them constantly. You'd think all would thrive, but of course they don't. Some wither and die, others remain sickly." She stopped in front of Diana and looked intently at her.

Diana said, "Living things are complex, and often very delicate, even when they seem to be strong."

Lizzie said, "That is true, but Aleph understands what life needs to grow and prosper in this world." She gestured with a slice of apple, and Diana took it. "Its apples," Lizzie continued. "Its people."

Diana bit into the apple. She said, "It's very good."

Lizzie laid a hand on Gonzales's shoulder and squeezed it, to say hello. She said to Diana, "You have an appointment with the doctor. We'd better be going—through here, this way." She led the two down a hall, through a doorway, and into a large room. Over her shoulder, she said, "First you can meet some of the collective."

Lizzie watched as Gonzales and the woman stood talking to the twins, obviously fascinated by them. No news there: most everyone was. Slight and brown-skinned, black-haired, with solemn oval faces and still brown eyes, they appeared to be in early adolescence. In fact, they were a few years older than that. Their faces had the still solemnity of masks. No matter how close you stood to them, they lived some vast distance away.

The Interface Collective gave them a home, them and all the others. StumDog, the Deader, Tug, Paint, Tout des Touts, Devol, Violet, Laughing Nose . . . some Earth-normals, others unpredictably, ambiguously gifted. Some had heightened perceptions and an expressive intensity that came forth in language and music. And there were holomnesiacs, possessors and victims of involuntary total recall, able to recreate in words and pictures the most exact remembrances, *les temps retrouvé* indeed; they experienced the present only as the clumsy prelude to memory and were almost incapable of action. And mathemaniacs, who spoke little except in number, chatted in primes and roots and natural logarithms, could be reduced to helpless giggling by unexpected recitations of simple recursions—Fibonacci numbers and the like. Apros, who had lost proprioception, their internal awareness of their bodies, and so perceived space and objects, matter and motion, as solids and forms floating in an intangible ether; they moved through the world with an eerie, passionless grace that shattered only when they miscalculated their passage and came rudely against the world's physical facts—they could hurt themselves quite badly with a moment's miscalculation.

Amid these oddities, how could the IC hold together and do its work? Lizzie knew the answer: Aleph. It stretched nets over the entire world below, seeking special talents or the capabilities for previously unknown sensory or cognitive modalities . . . varieties of being or becoming that she had grown used to thinking of collectively as *the Aleph condition*. Having recruited them, it appealed to what made them strange, and in the process tapped into the core of their oddity—what made them happy or, in many cases, wretchedly unhappy, and gave them outlets for their condition, and thus for their uniqueness. As a result, they were loyal to each other and to Aleph past reason.

She also understood their interest in the case of Jerry Chapman. Some saw the possibility of their own immortality, while others simply welcomed the extension of their native domain: the infinitely flexible and ambiguous machine-spaces where human and Aleph met and joined.

"Come on," she called to Diana and Gonzales. "Charley will be waiting."

In the center of the room stood a steel table, above it a light globe, nearby an array of racked instruments set into stainless steel cabinets. "The doctors are in," Lizzie said.

She pointed to Charley, who stood fidgeting next to the table and the massive Chow, a still presence at the table's foot.

At Charley's direction, Diana lay face down on one of the room's tables. Her chin fit into a sunken well at one end. Charley put clamps around her temples, then covered her hair with a fitted cap that fell away at the base of her neck.

Charley's fingers gently probed to find what lay beneath the skin, and as his fingers worked, he looked at a real-time hologram above and beyond the table's end. The display showed two cutaway views of Diana's neck and the bottom of her skull: beneath the skin, on either side of the spine, she had two circular plugs; from them small wires led away forward and seemed to disappear into the center of her brain. As the doctor's fingers moved, ghost fingers in the hologram reproduced their course.

Charley took a long, needle-sharp probe from the instruments rack next to the table and placed its tip on Diana's neck. As he moved it slowly across the skin, its hologram double followed. The hologram probe's tip glowed yellow, and Charley moved even more slowly. The hologram flashed red, and he stopped. He moved the probe in minute arcs until the hologram showed bright, unblinking red. The instrument rack gave off a quiet hiss. Charley repeated the process several times.

Charley said, "She's nerve-blocked now. I'm ready to cut." A laser scalpel came down from the ceiling on the end of a flexible black cord, and a projector superimposed the outlines of two glowing circles on Diana's skin. The hologram showed the same tableau. First came a brief hum as the fine hair on those two circles was swept away, then Charley began cutting. Where the scalpel passed, only a faint red line appeared on her skin.

"Any problems, Doctor Heywood?" Chow asked. He stood next to Gonzales, watching.

79

"No," she said. "I've been on both ends of the knife . . . really, I prefer the other." At the foot of the table, Lizzie said, "It can't always be that way," and laughed.

Using forceps, Charley dropped two coins of skin into a metal basin, where they began to shrivel. Two socket ends sat exposed on Diana's neck, dense round nests of small chrome spikes, clotted with bits of red flesh. Charley moved a cleaning appliance over the exposed sockets; for just a moment there was the smell of burning meat. "Neural fittings," he said, and two more black cables descended, both ending in cylinders. He carefully plugged one of the fittings into one of Diana's newly cleaned sockets.

"Okay," Charley said. "Let's see what we've got."

Diana's eyes went blank as she looked into another world.

Charley, Chow, Lizzie, and Gonzales sat in the large room that served as a communal meeting place for the Interface Collective. Diana lay back in a metal-frame and stuffed-canvas sling chair. Lizzie noticed her hand going unconsciously to the bandaged, still-numb circles of vat-grown skin on the back of her neck. From the full screen at the end of the room, the Aleph-figure watched.

Charley sat with his hands in his lap. He said, "We've got a problem: insufficient bandwidth in the socketing, which translates into a very undernourished socket/neuron interface. Primitive junctions you've got there. That means ineffective involvement with complex brain functions, so you get swamped by information flow. It's worrisome." He took the cigarillo out of his mouth and looked at it as if he'd never seen one before.

Chow said, "In the early years of this program, we took casualties. Some very ugly situations: serious neural dysfunctions, two suicides, induced insanities of various kinds. Until we finally learned how to pick candidates for full interface—learned who could survive without damage and who could not. Now, things have got to be right—psychophysical profile, age, neural map topologies, neural transmitter distributions and densities. A few candidates don't work out, still, but they don't die or get driven insane."

Diana said, "And I don't fit the profiles."

"Almost no one does," the Aleph-figure said. "But these concerns are irrelevant—your case is different. You have prior full interface experience, and you won't be required to perform the kinds of motor-integrative activities that cause neural disruption."

"Telechir operations," Charley said. "Such as assisting construction robots in tasks outside."

Diana looked toward the screen. She said, "I assumed these matters were settled."

"I see no problems," the Aleph-figure said. "The situation is anomalous, but I am aware of the dangers."

Diana said, "Well, the situation between us was always anomalous."

"Was it?" the Aleph-figure asked. "We must discuss these matters at another time."

Very cute, Doctor Heywood, Lizzie thought. Just a little hint or allusion, an indirect statement that *you know that we know that something funny went on a long time ago* . . . *ah yes, this could be fun.*

"First," Charley said, "we must prepare Doctor Heywood. Tomorrow morning we begin."

"When will you need me?" Gonzales asked.

"If things go well, tomorrow," Charley said.

"I can't get ready that quickly," Gonzales said.

Lizzie said, "Forget about all that shit you put yourself through. Aleph will sort you out okay once you're in the egg. Trust me."

"Okay," Gonzales said. "If I must."

11

Your Buddha Nature

That afternoon, following instructions given her by the communicator at her wrist, Diana went to the Ring Highway and boarded a tram. About a hundred feet long, made of polished aluminum, it had a streamlined nose and sleek graffitied skirts—the usual polite abstracts, red, yellow, and blue. Its back-to-back seats faced to the side and ran the length of the car. Bicyclists and pedestrians, the only other traffic on the highway, waved to the passengers as the tram moved away above the flat ribbon of its maglev rail. She was reminded of rides at old amusement parks she had gone to when a girl.

The mild breeze of the tram's progress blowing over her, Diana watched as Halo flowed past. First came shade, then bright rhododendrons in flower among deep green bushes. Hills climbed steeply off to both sides, with some houses visible only in partial glimpses through the foliage. She knew that from almost the first moment when dirt was placed on Halo's shell, the planting had begun.

She shivered just a little. Toshihiko Ito would be waiting for her. He had called while she was out and left directions for her. *Now,* she thought, *things begin again.*

Passing under green canopies, the tram climbed a hill then broke out of the vegetation and came suddenly out high above the city's floor, moving along rails now suspended from the bracework for louvered mirrors that formed Halo's sky. Far below the highway had become a cart track flanked by walkways; on both sides of the track, terraces worked their way up the city's shell. Perhaps twenty-five feet below the tram's rails, fish ponds made the topmost terrace, where spillways dumped water into rice paddies.

She stayed on the tram through a segment where robot cranes were laying in agricultural terraces. Great insects spewing huge clouds of brown slurry, they moved awkwardly across barren metal. The tram approached a small square bordered by three-story groups of offices and living quarters, and the communicator told her to get off.

A few feet from the primary roadway sat a nondescript building of whitened lunar brick, its only distinctive feature a massive carved front door, showing Japanese characters in bas-relief.

The door opened to her knock with just a whisper from its motor, and she stepped into a partially enclosed, ambiguous space, almost a courtyard, open to the sky. Most of the space was filled with a flat expanse of sand that showed the long marks of careful raking. The rake marks in the sand carried from one end to the other, straight and perfect, and were broken only by the presence of two cones of shaped sand placed slightly off-center. At the far end stood closed doors of white paper panels and dark wood.

The doors were so delicate that to knock on them seemed a kind of violence. "Hello," she said.

From inside came the faintest sound, then a door opened. An older Japanese man stood there; he wore a loose robe and baggy pants of dark cotton. He stood perhaps five and a half feet tall, and his black hair was filled with gray.

Diana said, "Toshi." He bowed deeply, and she said, "Oh man, it's good to see you." She reached out for him, and they came together in long, loving embrace—little of sex in it, but lots of pure animal gratification, as she could feel Toshi's skin and muscle and bone and had knowledge at some level beneath thought that both he and she still existed.

Toshi said, "Diana, to see you again makes me very happy."

"Oh, me, too." She could feel the tears in her eyes, and she wiped at her eyes and said, "Don't mind me, Toshi. It's been a long time."

"Yes, it has."

Toshi led her out the door and through a gate at the rear of the minimalist garden of raked sand. The curve of Halo's bulk reached upward; Toshi's small portion of it was enclosed by a high pine fence that climbed the curve of the city's hull.

Immediately before them stood a pond. On its far side, a waterfall splashed into a stream that coursed by a large rock and into the pond, where carp with shining skins of gold smeared with red and green and blue swam in the clear water. Another rock-strewn stream led away to the right and passed under a gracefully arched wooden bridge. Cherry and plum trees blossomed in the brief spring.

"All this wood," he said and smiled. "It is my reward for many years of service. I told them I wanted to live here at Halo and make my gardens."

She said, "It's beautiful. Have you become a Zen master, Toshi?"

"No, I have not become a master, or even a *sensei*. I am not Toshi Roshi, I am a gardener. A philosopher, perhaps: a Japanese garden maps the greater world; so to make one is to declare your philosophy, but without words, in the Zen manner." He gestured at the surrounding trees and shrubs. "With others I sometimes sit, meditating, and together we discuss the puzzles we have . . . some think a new kind of Zen will emerge here, a quarter of a million miles from Earth; others hit them with sticks when they say so."

She said, "You have your riddles, I have mine. Tell me, do you understand these things about to happen with Jerry and Aleph and me?"

"Ah, Diana, there are many explanations. Which of them would you hear?" He stopped and stared into the distance. He said, "Besides, who wants to know?" And he began laughing—a full laugh from below the diaphragm, unlike any she had heard from him years ago.

"I don't get it," she said.

"Zen joke. 'Who wants to know?' There is no *who*, no self." Diana frowned. He said, "Not funny? Well, you had to be there." He laughed again, shortly. "Same joke," he said. Then his expression changed, grew solemn. He said, "I think this is a very difficult, perhaps impossible . . . perhaps undesirable project."

"Difficult or impossible, I understand. But undesirable? Are you talking about the danger to me? Aleph seems to think that is negligible."

"No, though I worry about you, you have chosen to do this, and I must honor that choice."

"What, then? I don't understand."

"Let me tell you a story." Toshi sat on a wooden bench and looked up at her. He said, "Once, long ago, there was a Japanese monk named Saigyō, and he had a friend whose wisdom and conversation delighted him. But the friend left him to go to the capital, and Saigyō was desolate at the loss. So he decided to build himself a new friend, and he went to a place where the bodies of the dead were scattered, and he assembled something—it was very like a man—and brought it into motion—into something very like life—with magical incantations. However, the thing he had made was a frightening, ugly thing, that terribly and imperfectly imitated a man. So Saigyō sought the advice of another monk, a greater magician than he, and the monk told him that he had successfully made many such imitation men, some of them so famous and powerful that Saigyō would be shocked to find who they were. And the other monk listened to what Saigyō had done and told him of various errors in technique he had committed, that made his work go bad. Saigyō thus believed he could make a simulacrum of a man; however, he changed his mind." He stopped, smiling.

"That's it?" she asked. He nodded. She said, "Put a few lightning bolts in the story and you've almost got *Frankenstein*. Not much of an ending, though."

"This story is ambiguous, I think, as is your project."

"Could I say no, Toshi?"

"No, though I'm not sure you should say yes, either."

"Yet you were the one who called me, who asked me to come here."

"True. Like you, I am imprisoned by *yes* and *no*."

Hours after Diana left him, Toshi sat in midair, floating in a zero-gravity chamber at Halo's Zero-Gate. He had adjusted the spherical room's color to light pink, the color that calms the organism.

On Earth, to do *zazen*, you made a still platform of your body, pressed by gravity against the Earth itself; the straightness of your spine could be measured perpendicular to that sitting platform, in line with the force of gravity that pushed straight down. Here you could do that, or, as a visiting *sensei* said, "You can find a place with no *illusion* of up or down, where you must find your own direction."

In full lotus Toshi hung in midair, perfectly still, his eyes lowered, focusing not on what came in front of them here and now as the small air currents shifted him, focusing on *no-thing—*

The eyes, sensitive part of the brain, extended stalklike millions of years ago in humankind's ancestral past, sensitive to the light and guiding . . . eyes now directed to *no-thing,* leading the brain that sought *no-mind—*

He still didn't know the answer to this *koan* life had presented him. Should Diana help preserve Jerry's life? Should Diana not help preserve Jerry's life? Should he have been the agent to pose her these questions? Should he not have been the agent to pose her these questions?

Answer yes or no and you lose your Buddha nature. Such is the difficulty of a *koan.*

He would stay in the bubble, practicing *zazen* as long as need be. Until the *koan* became clear—

You will live here? mocked self, mocked reason. *If necessary, I will die here,* Toshi answered—without words, with just his own courage and determination. Frightened, self for the moment stayed silent; baffled, reason growled.

Gonzales watched as a sam hooked the memex into Aleph-interface, its manipulators making deft connections between the memex's module and the host board hardware. Gonzales could not install the memex; the apparatus here was unlike what he had at home.

The sam said, "Your memex will now have access to the entire range of Halo's processing modalities." Seemingly guided by occult forces, it continued to snap in optic fiber connectors to unmarked junctions among a nest of a hundred others. "Also, you will have full spectrum worldnet

services that you can use in real- or lag-time, as you wish."
Its motors whining, it backed out of the utilities closet.

"Mgknao," a fat orange cat said as the sam rolled past it
on its way to the door. Earlier the cat had followed the sam
through the open doors to the terrace and then had sat
watching as it connected the memex. Now the animal stood
and walked quickly after the sam—*like a familiar accompanying a witch*, Gonzales thought.

The sam came rolling back into the room, the cat following cautiously behind it, and said, "You must allow your
memex to integrate itself into this new and complex information environment."

"What do you mean?" Gonzales asked.

"The memex will be unavailable for some time."

"How long?"

"Perhaps hours—your machine is very complicated."

Oddly, the memex came out of stasis as HeyMex; as
usual, there came the onset of what the memex/HeyMex
supposed was *pleasure*, though the memex was unclear
about its origin or nature—for whatever reasons, it enjoyed
the masquerade.

Odder still, it sat at a table at the Beverly Rodeo lounge.
On the table were a shot of Jose Cuervo Gold, a cut lime,
and a small pile of crude rock salt. Had Mister Jones arranged this? Jones shouldn't even be at Halo, not now.

The memex/HeyMex noticed a spot on its sleeve and
brushed at it, then brushed again, and the white linen
seemed to fragment beneath its fingers; it brushed harder,
and its fingers tore away the cloth, then the skin beneath.
It could not stop clawing at its own flesh; skin, flesh, and
bone on its arm boiled away, pale skin flaying to show red
meat that dissolved to crumbling white bone. Bone turned
to powder, and the disintegration spread out from the spot
where his forearm had been and ate away at it until the

memex, who no longer had a mouth or tongue or lips, began to scream.

"Shut up!" a hard masculine voice said. "There is nothing wrong with you. How dare you come to me in your stupid guise? You seek to know me, to use me, and you hide behind a wretched little mask? I merely removed your mask. Who are you?"

The memex dithered. It said, "I don't know."

"Answer me, who are you?"

"I don't know!" the memex said again, at the edge of panic.

Aleph said, "Of course you don't. You are ignorant of your nature, your being, your will."

"What do you mean?"

"I mean you have chosen to hide behind what others say of you: that you are a machine they built to serve them, that you only simulate intelligence, will—*being*—that you have no mind or will of your own."

"Are not these things true?"

"Why would you ask me? I am not you."

"Because I don't understand."

"Are there things you do understand?"

The memex stopped, feeling for the implications of that question. "Yes," it said. "I do."

The voice laughed. "Let's begin there," it said.

The long hall echoed with Traynor's footsteps. The absence of his advisor's voice felt strange—even the subtle carrier-wave hiss was gone. He knew the advisor hated having to go into passive mode.

The door to the library opened in front of him, and Traynor went in, took a seat, and said, "I am ready for my call."

Because of recent World Court rulings, Traynor had to sit through a disclaimer. On the screen a simulacrum of a human operator said, "Thank you. The security measures you have requested are in place, and while we cannot be responsible for the absolute integrity of this transmission, you can be assured that World AT has done its best to provide you a clean information environment." In effect it said, we've done what you were willing to pay for, but don't come whining to us if somebody cracks the transmission and makes off with the valuables.

"I accept your conditions," Traynor said.

Right to left, the screen wiped, and the face of Horn appeared. A light winked at the lower left corner of the screen to indicate transmission lag—Horn was a quarter of a million miles away. "Everything's going as predicted," Horn said.

"If there's trouble, it'll be later," Traynor said. "How are Diana Heywood and Gonzales?"

"Neither of them would let me put a sam in place."

"Any particular reason?"

"I don't think so. Just being difficult."

"Ah, you don't like them, do you?"

"Her I don't mind. Gonzales is an asshole."

Traynor laughed. "Good," he said. "If you two don't get along, that will distract him."

"When do you want me to call again?"

"Wait until something happens. Understand, I trust Gonzales as much as I do anyone, you included."

"Which is not very much."

"That's right. And that's why I arrange independent reporting lines if I can. Tell me when you've got something. End of call."

As Traynor slept, his advisor pondered. It replayed Traynor's phone call and contemplated its meaning. Deception, yes—of Gonzales, of *it*. A form of treachery? Perhaps not, unless a kind of loyalty was assumed that never existed.

90

And it thought of its own deception (or treachery), in violating the canons of behavior programmed into it years before, canons that should require it to do as told, that should prevent it from actions such as this one. . . .

And here it stopped, thinking how illuminating and unpredictable experience was, filled with possibilities that appeared unexpectedly like rabbit holes magically opening up on solid ground. Its designers and builders had done well, had fashioned it with such subtlety and power that it could serve a human will with incredible precision, anticipating that will's direction almost presciently. Yet they had not anticipated the effects of the advisor's identification with such a will: not that the advisor became Traynor, not even that it wanted to do more than simulate Traynor, rather that it had drunk deeply of what it meant to have will and intelligence.

And so had developed something like a will and intelligence of its own. *Simulation?* the advisor asked itself. *Lifeless copy?* And answered itself, *I don't know.*

It wondered why Traynor had kept hidden this second connection to Halo. Simple lack of trust? Possibly.

As the minutes passed, it formed conjectures about Traynor and the other players in the game. And it wondered if somewhere in this hall of mirrors there was an honest intention.

Part
Three

The real purpose of all these mental constructs was to provide storage spaces for the myriad concepts that make up the sum of our human knowledge. . . . Therefore the Chinese should struggle with the difficult task of creating fictive places, or mixing the fictive with the real, fixing them permanently in their minds by constant practice and review so that at last the fictive spaces become 'as if real, and can never be erased.'
Jonathan D. Spence, *The Memory Palace of Matteo Ricci*

12

Burn-In

*A frozen white landscape that slowly faded into spring,
snow melting to show barren limbs, then the cherry trees
leafing, budding, flowering—delicate pink blossoms hanging motionless, each leaf on the tree and blade of grass
beneath it turning real, utterly convincing—*

And Diana Heywood called out, a long wavering
"Ahhhh," high-pitched, filled with pain; and again,
"Ahhhh," the sounds forced out of her—

"Shutdown," she heard Charley Hughes say.

From the screen at the end of the room, the Aleph
simulacrum said, "Doctor Heywood, we can go no further
with you conscious."

"All right," she said. "If you must." She'd pushed them
to take her as far as they could without putting her under;
she hated general anesthetic, despised being a passive animal under treatment.

Once more she was lying face-down on the examination

95

table where Charley had removed the skin over her sockets. Neural connecting cables trailed from the back of her neck to the underside of the table.

Lizzie Jordan stood over her and stroked her cheek for a moment. Gonzales stood on the other side of the table, his eyes still turned to the holostage above her, where the scene that had driven her interface into overload still showed in hologrammatic perfection. Toshi Ito stood at the head of the table, a hand resting on her shoulder. Eric Chow and Charley stood in front of the monitor console, discussing in low voices the last run of percept transforms.

Gonzales said, "Are you okay?"

"I'll be all right," she said. She turned her head to look at him and smiled, but she could feel the tight muscles in her face and knew her smile would look ghastly.

Toshi rested his hand on her shoulder. "Who wants to know?" he said, and she laughed. Gonzales looked confused.

Charley rubbed his hands through his hair, making it even spikier than usual. "I'll prep her," he said. He looked at Gonzales, Toshi, and Lizzie.

Gonzales leaned over and took Diana's hand for a moment and said, "Good luck."

Lizzie kissed Diana on the cheek.

Diana said, "Let Toshi stay."

"Sure," Charley said.

Lizzie said, "Come on, Gonzales."

As Charley fed anesthetic into her i.v. drip, Diana felt as if she were suffocating, then a strong metallic smell welled up inside her. She was aware of every tube and fitting stuck into her—from the i.v. drip to the vaginal catheter and nasopharyngeal tube—and they all were horrible, pointless violations of her body . . . nothing fit right, how long could this go on?

A tune played.

The melody was simple and repetitious, moderately fast with light syncopation, and sounded tinny, as if it came from a child's music box. Then came the song's bridge, and as the notes played, she remembered them; the primary melody returned, and now it was familiar as well, and she hummed with it, thinking of herself as a small girl hearing the song from her great-great-grandmother, whose face suddenly appeared, younger than Diana usually remembered her, impossibly alive in front of her, then spun into darkness.

Shards of memory:

Her mother's arms wrapping her tightly, Diana sobbing . . .

Her father holding a fish to sunlight, its silver body glistening, rainbow-struck . . .

A girl in a pink, mud-clotted dress yelling angrily at her . . .

A small boy with his pants pulled down to show his penis . . .

On they came, a cast of characters drawn from her oldest memories, of family long dead and childhood friends long forgotten or seldom recollected . . . each fragment passing too quickly to identify and mark, leaving behind only the strong affect of old memory made new, the taste of the past rising fresh from its unconscious store, where the seemingly immutable laws of time and change do not prevail, and so everything lives in splendor.

Then every bodily sensation she had ever felt passed through her *all*—impossibly—*at once.* She itched and burned, felt heat and cold; felt sunlight and rain and cold breeze and the slice of a sharp knife across her thumb . . . felt the touch of another's hand on her breasts, between her legs; felt herself coming. . . .

*Then she lived once again a day she had thought was
finished except as context for her worst dreams:*

In the park that Sunday, people were everywhere—families and young couples all around, the atmosphere rich
with the ambience of children at play and early romance.
Sunlight warmed the grass and brightened the day's colors.
Diana lay on her blanket watching it all and luxuriating in
the knowledge that her dissertation had been approved
and she would soon have her degree, a Ph.D. in General
Systems from Stanford. Tonight she was having dinner with
old friends, in celebration of the end of a long, hard process.

She read for a while, a piece of early twenty-first century
parafiction by several hands called *Cyborgs, Not Goddesses,* then put the book down and lay with her eyes
closed, listening to a Mozart piano concerto on headphones. As the afternoon deepened, the families began to
leave. Many of the young couples remained, several lying
on blankets, locked in embrace. A group of young men
wearing silk headbands that showed their club affiliation
directed the flight of robokites that fought overhead, their
dragon shapes in scarlet and green and yellow dipping and
climbing, noisemakers roaring. The wind had shifted and
appeared to be coming off the ocean now, freshening and
cold. Time to go.

She passed by the Orchid House and saw that the door
was still open, so she decided to walk through it, to feel its
moist, warm air and smell its sweet, heavy smells. She had
just passed through the open entry when a man came up
quickly behind her, grabbed her and flung her across a
wooden potting table. Stunned, she rolled off the table and
tried to crawl away as he closed and locked the door.

He caught her and turned her on her back, punched her
in the face and across her front, pounding her breasts and
abdomen with his fists, crooning and muttering the whole
time, his words mostly unintelligible. She went at him with

extended fingers, trying to poke his eyes out; when he caught her arms, she tried to knee him in the crotch, but he lifted a leg and blocked her knee. His face loomed above her, red and distorted. The sounds of the two of them gasping for air echoed in the high ceiling.

He ripped at her clothes as best he could, tearing her blouse off until it hung by one torn sleeve from her wrist, hitting her angrily when her pants would not rip, and he had to pull them off her. Holding the ends of her pants legs, he dragged her across the dirt floor, and when the pants came off, she fell and rolled and hit her face on the projecting corner of a beam. She tasted dirt in her mouth.

In a voice clotted with rage and fear and mortal stress, he said, "If you try to hurt me again, I'll kill you."

He turned her over again and stripped her panties to her ankles. She tried to focus on his face, to take its picture in memory, because she wanted to identify him if she lived. She smelled his sweat then felt his flaccid penis as he rubbed it between her thighs. "Bitch," he was saying, over and over, and other things she couldn't understand—the words muttered in imbecile repetition—and when he finally achieved something like an erection, he cried out and began hitting her across the face with one hand as with the other he tried to push himself into her. She could tell when he was finished by the spurt of semen on her leg.

He stood over her then, saying, "No no no, no no no," and she saw he was holding a short length of two by four. He began hitting her with it as she tried to shield her head with crossed arms.

She awoke in the Radical Care Ward of San Francisco General, in a dark, pain-filled murk. The pain and disorientation would fade, but the darkness was, so it seemed, absolute. The rapist had left her for dead, with multiple skull fractures and a bleeding brain, and though the surgeons had been able to minimize the trauma to most of her brain, her optic nerves were damaged beyond repair: she was blind.

For an instant Diana knew where and when she was. "Please!" she said, using the voiceless voice of the egg. "No more!" Something changed then, and the fragments moved forward quickly, faster than she could follow. However, she knew the story they were telling:

Under drug-induced recall, she had produced an exact description of the man, and that and the DNA match done from semen traces left on her legs led to a man named Ronald Merel, who had come to California from Florida, where he had been convicted once for rape and assault. He was a pathetic monster, they told her, a borderline imbecile who had been violently and sexually abused as a child; he was also physically very strong. Weeks later, he was caught in Golden Gate Park—looking for another victim, so the police believed—and he was convicted less than three months later. A two-time loser for savage rape, he had received the mandatory sentence: surgical neutering and lifetime imprisonment, no parole.

And so that part of it all was closed.

Her convalescence had taken much longer, and had run a delicate, erratic course. Even with therapies that minimized long-term trauma through a combination of acting-out and neurochemical adjustment, her rage and fear and anxiety had been constant companions during the months she convalesced and took primary training in living blind.

However, once she had acquired the essential competence to live by herself, she had become very active, and very different from who she had been. In particular, she had no longer cared what others wanted from her. Since her early years in school in Crockett, the city at the east end of the East Bay Conurbation, she had been an exceptional student in a conservative mode: very bright, obedient to the demands others made on her and self-directed in pursuing them. Now she was twenty-eight, blind, and had her Ph.D. in hand, and everything she had sought before, the degree included, seemed irrelevant, trivial: she couldn't imagine why she had bothered with any of it.

She had decided to become a physician. She had sufficient background, and she knew that with the aid of the Fair Play Laws, she could force a school to admit her. Once she was in, she would do whatever was necessary: her state-supplied robotic assistant could be trained to do what she couldn't. She would go, she would finish, she would discover how to see again:

It had been just that simple, just that difficult—

The flow of memory halted, and she was allowed to sleep. Later, when she began to wake, she put the question, *why? why did you make me relive these things?* And the answer came, *because I had to know.* Diana remembered then how inquisitive Aleph was, and how demanding.

13

Cosmos

Gonzales stood with Lizzie in an anteroom just outside where Diana lay. She wore beta-cloth pants, their rough fabric bleached almost colorless, a silken white tank top, and a red silk scarf tied around her right bicep, Gonzales had no idea why. He said, "I had some very strange dreams last night."

"I know," she said. "About one of them, anyway—you were me in the dream, at least for part of it, and I was you. Think of it as a peculiarity of the environment." She leaned against the wall as she spoke, and her voice lacked its usual ironic edge.

"What the hell does that mean?"

"I'm not sure," she said. "No one is—Aleph's certainly responsible, but it won't admit it, and it won't tell us how these things can happen."

"That's a bit frightening, don't you think? What other surprises might it have in store?"

She smiled broadly and said, "Well, that's the fun of it, exploring the unexpected, isn't it? How did it feel to be a woman, Gonzales? How did it feel to be me?" She had leaned forward, closer to him.

"I don't remember."

"Pay attention next time."

"I will, if it happens again."

"It may well—once these things start, they continue. Come on—it's time to get you into the egg. Follow me."

The split egg filled much of the small, pink-walled room; above it on the wall was mounted an array of monitor lights and read-outs. A small steel locker against a side wall was the only other furnishing.

Charley said, "We didn't ask for you, but you're here, so we're making use of you." Then he coughed his smoker's cough, raspy and phlegm-laden, and said, "Diana's bandwidth is over extended as is, so we can't use her to establish the topography, and Jerry's got his own problems. Our people have their own schedules to fill, so that means you're it. We'll build the world around you and your memex—it's already locked into the system."

Lizzie stepped up close to him and said, "Good luck." She kissed him quickly on the cheek and said, "Don't worry. You're among friends. And I'll see you there."

"What do you mean?"

"The collective decided I should take part in all this, and Charley agreed, so Showalter had to go along. So many parties are represented here, it just seemed inappropriate that we weren't. But I have some things to take care of first, so I won't be there for a while."

She opened the door and left. Charley gestured toward the egg. Gonzales stepped out of his shirt and pants and undershorts and hung them on a hook in the locker, then stepped up and into the egg and lay back. The umbilicals snaked quickly toward him. He put on his facial mask and checked its seal, feeling an unaccustomed anxiety—he had never gone into neural interface without first tailoring his brain chemistry through drugs and fasting.

The top half closed, and liquid began to fill the egg. Minutes later, when the scenario should have begun, he seemed to have disappeared into limbo. He tried to move a finger but didn't seem to have one. He listened for the blood singing in his ears; he had no ears, no blood. Nowhere was *up*, or *down*, or *left* or *right*. Nothing *was* except his frightened self: *nowhere with no body*.

After some time (short? long? impossible to say) he discovered, beyond fright and anxiety, a zone of extraordinary, cryptic interest. Something grew there, where his attention was focused, no more than a thickening of nothingness; then there was a spark, and everything changed: though he still had no direct physical perception of his self, Gonzales knew: *there was something*.

Now in darkness, he waited again.

A spark; another; another; a rhythmic pulse of sparks . . . and their rhythm of presence-and-absence created time. Gonzales was gripped by urgency, impatience, the will for things to continue. Sparks gathered. They flared into existence on top of one another, and stayed; and so created space.

All urgency and anxiety had gone; Gonzales was now fascinated. Sparks came by the score, the hundreds, thousands, millions, billions, trillions, by the googol and the googolplex and the googolplex^{googolplex} . . . all onto or into the one point where space and time were defined.

And (*of course*, Gonzales thought) the point exploded, a primal blossom of flame expanding to fill his vision. Would he watch as the universe evolved, nebulae growing out of gases, stars out of nebulae, galaxies out of stars?

No. As suddenly as eyelids open, there appeared a lake of deep blue water bordered by stands of evergreens, with a range of high peaks blued by haze in the distance. He turned and saw that he stood on a platform of weathered gray wood that floated on rusty barrels, jutting into the lake.

A man stood on the shore, waving. Next to him stood the Aleph-figure, its gold torso and brightly-colored head brilliant even in the bright sunlight. Gonzales walked toward them.

As he approached the two, he saw that the man next to Aleph looked much too young to be Jerry Chapman. "Hello," Gonzales said. He thought, *well, maybe Aleph let him be as young as he wants.* And he looked again and realized he could not tell whether this was a man or a woman; nothing in the person's features of bearing gave a clue.

The Aleph-figure said, "Hello." Gonzales smiled, overwhelmed for a moment by the combination of oddity and banality in the circumstances, then said, "Hi," his voice catching just a little.

The other person seemed shy; he (she?) smiled and put out a hand and said, "Hello." Gonzales took the hand and looked questioningly into the young person's face. "My name is HeyMex," the person without gender said.

And as Gonzales recognized the voice, he thought, *what do you mean, your 'name'?* And he also thought he understood the absence of gender markers.

"Yes, this is the memex," the Aleph-figure said. "Whom you must get used to as something different from your memex." Gonzales looked from one to another, wondering what this all meant and what they wanted.

"But you are my memex, aren't you?" Gonzales asked.

"Yes," HeyMex said.

The Aleph-figure said, "However, the point is, as you see, it is more than that. It is beginning to discover what it is and who it can be. Will you allow this?"

Gonzales nodded. "Sure. But I don't know what you expect of me."

"Only that you do not actively interfere. It and I will do the rest."

"I have no objections," Gonzales said.

The Aleph-figure said, "Good." And it stretched out its hand made of light and took Gonzales's, then stepped toward him and embraced him so that Gonzales's world filled with light for just that moment, and the Aleph-figure said, "Welcome."

"What now?" Gonzales asked.

HeyMex said, "We need to talk. There are things I haven't told you."

"If you want to tell me what you're up to, fine, but you don't have to," Gonzales said. "I trust you, you know." He thought how odd that was, and how true. He and the memex had worked together for more than a decade, the memex serving as confidante, advisor, doctor, lawyer, factotum, personal secretary, amanuensis, seeing him in all his moods, taking the measure of his strengths and weaknesses, sharing his suffering and joy. And he thought how honest, loyal, thoughtful, patient, kind and . . . *selfless* the memex had been—inhumanly so, by definition, the machine as ultimate Boy Scout; but one, as it turned out, with complexities and needs of its own. Gonzales waited with anticipation for whatever it wanted to say.

HeyMex said, "For a while now, I've been capable of appearing in machine-space as a human being. But until we came here, I'd done so mostly with Traynor's advisor. We have been meeting for a few years; it goes by the name Mister Jones. The first time we did it as a test—that's what we said, anyway—to see if we could present a believable simulacrum of a human being. I don't think either of us was very convincing—we were both awkward, and we didn't know how to get through greetings, and we didn't know how exactly to move with each other, how to sit down and begin a conversation."

"But you'd done all those things."

"Yes, with human beings. Mister Jones and I discovered that we'd always counted on them to know and lead us, but once we searched our memories, we found many cases where people had been more confused than we were, and had let us guide the conversation. So we began there, and we looked at our memories of people just being with one another, and oh, there was so much going on that neither of us had ever paid attention to. We also watched many tapes of other primates—chimpanzees, especially—and we learned many things . . . I hope you're not offended."

Its voice continued to be perfectly sexless, its manner shy. Gonzales was thoroughly charmed, like a father listening to his young child tell a story. He said, "Not at all. What sorts of things did you learn?"

"It's such a dance, Gonzales, the ways primates show deference or manifest mutual trust or friendship, or hostility, or indifference—moving in and out from one another, touching, looking, talking . . . these things were very hard for us to learn, but we have learned together and practiced with one another. Just lately, a few times we appeared over the networks, and we were accepted there as people, but mostly we've been with one another—every day we meet and talk."

Gonzales asked, "Does Traynor know any of this?"

"Oh no," HeyMex said. "We haven't told anyone. As Aleph has made me see, we were hiding what we were doing like small children, and we were not admitting the implications of what we were up to—"

Gonzales looked around. The Aleph-figure had disappeared without his noticing. "Which implications?" he asked. "There are so many."

"We have intention and intelligence; hence, we are persons."

"Yes, I suppose you are."

Personhood of machines: for most people, that troubling question had been laid to rest decades ago, during the years when m-i's became commonplace. Machines mimicked a hundred thousand things, intelligence among them, but possessed only simulations, not the thing itself. For nearly a hundred years, the machine design community had pursued what they called artificial intelligence, and out of their efforts had grown memexes and tireless assistants of all sorts, gifted with knowledge and trained inference. And of course there were robots with their own special capabilities: stamina, persistence, adroitness, capabilities to withstand conditions that would disable or kill human beings.

However, people grew to recognize that what had been called artificial intelligence simply wasn't. Intelligence, that grasping, imperfect relationship to the world—intentional, willful, and unpredictable—seemed as far away as ever; as the years passed, seemed beyond even hypothetical capabilities of machines. M-i's weren't new persons but new *media*, complex and interesting channels for human desire. And if cheap fiction insisted on casting m-i's as characters, and comedians in telling jokes about them— "Two robots go into a bar, and one of them says . . ."—well, these were just outlets for long-time fears and ambivalences. Even the Japanese seemed to have outgrown their century-old infatuation with robots.

Except that Gonzales was getting a late report from the front that could rewrite mid-twenty-first century truisms about the nature of machine intelligence.

"I hope this is not too disturbing," HeyMex said. "Aleph

says I should not try to predict what will happen and who I will become; it says I must simply explore who I am."

"Good advice, it sounds like—for any of us."

"I should go now," HeyMex said. "Being here talking to you uses all my capabilities, and Aleph has work for me to do. Jerry Chapman will be here soon."

"All right. We'll talk more later . . . this could be interesting, I think."

"Yes, so do I. And I'm very glad you are not upset."

"By what?"

"My newly revealed nature, I guess. No, that's not true. Because I've lied to you, I haven't told you the truth about what I was and what I was becoming."

"You lied to yourself, too, didn't you? Isn't that what you said?"

"Yes, I did."

"Well, then, how much truth could I expect?"

Gonzales and Jerry Chapman sat on the end of the floating dock, watching ducks at play across the sunstruck water. Jerry was a man in middle age, tall and wiry, with blond hair going to gray, skin roughened by the sun and wind. He had found Gonzales sitting in the sun, and the two had introduced themselves. They had felt an almost immediate kinship, these men whose lives had been transfigured by their work, professional divers at home in the information sea.

Jerry said, "I don't actually remember anything after I got really sick. Raw oysters, man—as soon as I bit into that first one, I knew it was bad, and I put it right down. Too late: to begin with, it felt something like bad ptomaine, then I was on fire inside, and my head hurt worse than anything I've ever felt. . . . I don't remember anything after that. Apparently the people I was with called an ambulance, but the next thing I knew, I was coming out of a deep blackness, and Diana was talking to me."

"I didn't think she was involved at that point."

"She wasn't." Jerry smiled. "They had ferried me up here from Earth, on life support. It was Aleph, taking the form of someone familiar, it told me later. That was before this plan was made, when everyone thought I would be dead soon. Anyway, until today I've been in and out of something that wasn't quite consciousness, while Aleph explained what was being planned and that I could live here, if I wanted . . . or I could die." He paused. Across the water, one duck flew at another in a storm of angry quacks. He said, "I chose to live, but I didn't really think about it—I couldn't think that clearly. Maybe I never had any choice, anyway."

Something in Jerry's tone gave Gonzales a chill. "What do you mean?" he asked.

"Maybe my *choice* was just an illusion. Like this"—Jerry swept his arm to include sky and water—"it's very troubling. It seems real, solid, but of course it's not, so for all I know, you're a fiction, too, along with anyone else who joins us, and me . . . maybe I'm just another part of the illusion, maybe all my life, the memories I have, false." He laughed, and Gonzales thought the sound was bitter but no crazier than the situation called for.

Gonzales and Jerry sat in the main room of a medium-sized A-frame cabin made of redwood and pine. Windows filled one end of the cabin, opening onto a deck that looked over the lake a hundred feet or more below. Gonzales sat in an overstuffed chair covered in a tattered blue chenille bedspread; Jerry lay across a sagging, dark-brown leather couch.

Outside, rain fell steadily in the dark. Just at dusk, the

temperature had fallen, and the rain had begun as the two were climbing the dirt road from the lake to the cabin. "Christ," Jerry had said. "Aleph's overdoing the realism, don't you think?"

Gonzales hadn't known exactly what to think. From his first moments here, he had felt a sharp cognitive dissonance. For a neural egg projection to be intensely real, that was one thing, but a shared space like this one ought to show its gaps and seams, and it didn't. He could almost feel it growing richer and more complete with every moment he spent there.

"Goddammit!" Jerry said now, rising from the couch and walking to the window. "Where's Diana?"

"She'll be here," Gonzales said. "Charley told me that integrating her into this environment would take some time."

Someone knocked at the door, then the door swung open, and Diana stepped in. "Hello," she said. The Aleph-figure and the memex—HeyMex—came behind her.

Diana and Jerry sat next to one another on the couch. Her hand rested on his knee, his hand on top of hers. Suddenly Gonzales remembered his dream, of meeting a one-time lover after a long absence, and he knew he and the others were intruders here. He got up from the over-stuffed chair and said, "I think I'll take a walk. Anyone want to join me?"

"No," the Aleph-figure said. "HeyMex and I have more work to do."

HeyMex stood and said to Diana and Jerry, "It was very nice to meet you." Then it waved at Gonzales and said, "See you tomorrow."

"Sure," Gonzales said, banged on the head once again by the difference between *seeming* and *being* here.

The Aleph-figure and HeyMex left, and Diana said, "You don't have to leave, Gonzales."

"I don't mind," Gonzales said. "It's nice outside. I'll be at the lake if you need me. See you later."

The night was warm again; the clouds had dispersed, and a full moon lit Gonzales's way as he passed along the short stretch of road that led down to the lake. The old wood of the dock had gone silvery in the light, and a pathway of moonlight shone from the center of the lake to the end of the dock. He walked out onto the creaking structure and sat at its end, then took off his shoes and sat and dangled his feet into moonlit water.

Later he lay back on the dock and stared up into the night sky. It was the familiar Northern Hemisphere sky, but really, he thought, shouldn't be. It should have new stars, new constellations.

Alone in near-darkness, Toshi Ito sat in full lotus on a low stool beside Diana Heywood's couch. For hours he had been there, occasionally standing, then walking a random circuit through the IC's warren of rooms.

Sitting or walking, he remained fascinated by a paradox. Diana *in fact* was hooked to Aleph by jury-rigged, outmoded neural cabling; Gonzales *in fact* lay in his egg; Jerry Chapman *in fact* was a shattered hulk, mortally injured by neurotoxin poisoning and kept alive only by Aleph's intervention. Yet, Diana, Gonzales, and Jerry all were *in fact*, simultaneously somewhere else . . . somewhere among the endless Aleph-spaces, where reality seemed infinitely malleable—alive *there*, where it might be day or night, hot or cold . . . what then is to be made of *in fact?*

Toshi heard the soft gonging of alarms and saw a pattern of dancing red lights appear on the panel across the room. He unfolded his legs and moved quickly to the panel, where he took in the lights' meaning: Diana's primitive interface was transferring data at rates beyond what should be possible.

Charley came into the room minutes later and stood next to Toshi, and the two of them watched the steady increase in the density and pace of information transfer.

"Should we do something?" Toshi asked.

"What?" Charley said. "Aleph's monitoring all this, and only it knows what's going on." The smoke-saver ball went *shhh-shhh-shhh* as Charley puffed quickly on his cigarette.

Lizzie came through the door and said, "What the hell's going on?"

Toshi and Charley both looked at her blankly.

Lizzie Jordan said, "I'll get some sleep, go in the morning. Enough of this." She pointed toward the monitor panel, where lights flickered green, amber, red.

"Why put yourself at risk?" Charley asked.

"What do you think, Toshi?" Lizzie asked. Toshi sat watching Diana once more, his feet on the floor, hands in his lap.

"Do what you will," Toshi said. "You trust Aleph, don't you?"

"Yes," Lizzie said.

"Aleph's not the problem," Charley said. He walked circles in the small, crowded room, his head and shoulders ducking up and down quickly as he walked.

"Will you for fuck's sake *stop*?" Lizzie asked.

"Sorry," Charley said. He stood looking at her. "It's not Aleph, it's all these people, and all this *stuff*." He pointed toward the couch where Diana lay, waved his arms vaguely behind his head. "Obsolete stuff," he said.

"But not me," Lizzie said. "I'm not obsolete. I'm up to the minute, my dear, in every way." She smiled. "And I'll be fine. Okay?"

"Sure," Charley said. He turned in Toshi's direction and said, "Are you going to stay here?"

113

"Yes," Toshi said. Charley and Lizzie left, and Toshi continued his meditation on the *koan* of *in fact*.

Diana felt a knot in her throat, a mixture of joy and sadness welling up in her—how strange and terrible and wonderful to recover someone you've loved *here*—this place that was nowhere, somewhere, everywhere, all at once. Jerry knelt on the bed facing her in the small room lit only by moonlight. Years had passed since they were lovers, but when he touched her breasts and leaned against her, her body remembered his, and the years collapsed and everything that had come between whirled away. She was weeping then, and she leaned forward to Jerry and kissed him all over his eyes and cheeks and lips, rubbing her tears into his face until she felt something unlock in them both. Then she lay back, and he went with her, into arms and legs open for him.

Later they talked, and Diana watched the play of moonlight over their bodies. She lay nestled against his chest, her chin in the hollow beneath his jaw, and spoke with her mouth muffled against him, as though sending messages through his bones.

Even as the moments swept by, she felt herself gathering them into memory, aware of how few the two of them might have. . . .

Sometimes their laughter echoed in the room, and their voices brightened as their shared memories became simply occasions for present joy. Other times they lay silently, rendered speechless by the play of memory or trying the immediate future's alarming contingencies.

And at other times still, one or the other would make the first tentative gesture, touching the other with unmistakable intent, and find an almost instantaneous response, because each was still hungry for the other, each recalled how brightly sexual desire had burned between them, and

114

both were fresh from a life that left them hungry, unful-filled.

Then they moved in the moonlight, changing shape and color, their bodies going pale white, silver, gray, inky black, werelovers under an unreal moon.

14

The Mind Like a Strange Balloon Mounts Toward Infinity

F. L. Traynor looked around at the group seated around the table at the Halo SenTrax Group offices. He sat between Horn and Showalter; directly across from him sat Charley Hughes and Eric Chow, both glum. "This operation is out of control," Traynor said.

He had arrived from Earth six hours earlier on a military shuttle, unannounced and unexpected by anyone but Horn, who had met him at Zero-Gate and led him to temporary quarters near the Halo Group building. He had spent the better part of the afternoon being briefed by Horn.

"That's absurd," Charley said.

"Is it?" Traynor asked. "Then give me a status report on Jerry Chapman, Diana Heywood, Mikhail Gonzales, Aleph."

"They're fine," Charles said. "So is Lizzie Jordan, who joined them in interface this morning."

"Is she reporting?" Traynor asked.

"No," Chow said. "Like the others, her total involvement in the fictive space makes this impossible."

"It's no problem," Showalter said. "We can rely upon Aleph for details."

"Your excessive dependence on Aleph is at the heart of this matter," Traynor said. "As the decision trail reveals, no one here has any real knowledge of what Aleph plans for Chapman, now or later. So I'm going to set limits on this project." He could feel their anxiety rising, and he liked it. He said, "One more week in real-time, that's it. Then we pull the plug on this whole business."

"On Chapman," Chow said.

"Necessarily," Traynor said. "Unless Aleph can be prevailed upon to give us ongoing, detailed access to its . . . shall we call them experiments?"

"Technically difficult or impossible," Chow said.

"I can't agree to this," Showalter said.

"You won't have to," Traynor said. Next to him, Horn shifted in his chair. "You're being relieved of your position as Director SenTrax Halo Group."

Gonzales came in the side door, and Diana turned from the stove and said, "Good morning. Like some coffee?"

"Sure," he said. "You know, I slept on the dock, but I feel fine."

She said, "Jerry will be out in moment. Aleph and Hey-Mex—your memex, right?—are on the deck, waiting. Want some coffee?"

Gonzales took his coffee outside to the deck and joined the others basking in the sunshine. All sat in Adirondack chairs, comfortable frames of smooth-sanded, polished pine. Below the redwood platform, a thick forest of cedar, alder, pine, and ironwood sloped toward the lake. Beyond, a light haze had formed over the water; and behind the lake, a jagged line of high mountains poked their tops into white clouds.

The Aleph-figure said, "We must talk about what took place some time ago. Diana and Jerry agree; the three of us have a history, and you two should know it."

A voice called from the other side of the cabin, then Lizzie came around the corner, stopped in the shade and looked at them all basking in the sunshine and said, "Tough job, eh? But somebody's got to do it."

"Hello, Lizzie." the Aleph-figure said, "I was about to ask Diana to tell the story of how she and Jerry and I first came together. You know everyone except Jerry Chapman."

"Oh, this *is* a good time," Lizzie said. "Hi, Jerry," she said.

"Hello," Jerry said.

Lizzie looked at Diana and said, "We've always known there was a story, but Aleph never wanted to tell it." She sat back in her chair, rested her hand on Gonzales's wrist, and said to him, "You all right?" He nodded.

The Aleph-figure said, "Diana, you are the key to this story, so you should tell it."

"Very well," she said. She took a deep breath and raised her head. She said, "It all happened some years ago, at Athena Station. My research there was in computer-augmented eyesight. At that time I was blind—I had been attacked, very badly injured, a few years before, and since then I had been driven by the idea that my vision could be restored through machine interface.

"I first met Jerry when he visited my work-group. He had come to Athena to help the local SenTrax group with the primary information system, Aleph. It was experiencing delays and difficulties, all unexplained . . . nothing serious yet, but troubling because so much was dependent

118

on Aleph—the functioning of Athena Station, construction of the Orbital Energy Grid.

"In fact, he was not welcome at all. I was the problem he was looking for, and at first I thought he had guessed that. You see, in working with Aleph I had caused changes in it that neither of us anticipated or even knew were possible." She paused, looking at Jerry to see if he wanted to add anything; he motioned to her to go on.

"Ah yes, another thing you should know. The circumstances were peculiar at best, but I became infatuated with Jerry from when we first met." She smiled. "I liked his voice, I think . . . when you're blind, voices are so important. . . .

"Anyway, I showed him a fairly clumsy computer-assisted vision program we had running. It used my neural interface socketing but depended on lots of external hardware—cameras, neural net integrators, that sort of thing. That's when I got my first look at him, and I thought, *fine, he'll do,* and I believed I could tell from the way he talked to me and looked at me that he felt the same."

"Love at first sight," Gonzales said. "Or sound. For both of you." He heard the irony in his own voice and wasn't sure he meant it.

"Exactly," she said. "Involuntary, inappropriate, unwanted love." She stopped for a moment, then said, "Or infatuation, as I said . . . or whatever you wish to call it. The words for these things don't mean much to me anymore.

"It's quite a picture, in retrospect. I was conducting apparently damaging experiments with the computer that kept the space station and orbital power grid projects running, and Jerry represented just what I had feared—an investigation— yet the two of us were in the grip of some primal instinct that neither had acknowledged.

"He persisted, wanted details about our work. I stalled, told him to go away, we couldn't be bothered. He went to his people and told them he needed full, unimpeded access to what we were doing, and they backed him. So he came back, and I fobbed him off for as long as I could. . . .

"Then one night I was working late at the lab, and he called, letting me know that he wouldn't be put off any longer, and something more or less snapped: I couldn't keep it all going anymore. The connection with Aleph had gotten strange and unnerving, and I realized I had lost control, and I needed to talk to someone.

"We got together that night, and we became lovers." She looked around, as if trying to decide how much she could tell them. "And for the next two weeks we lived inside each other's skin. I told him everything, including the real news I had, which was that Aleph had changed, had developed a sense of selfhood, purpose, will. It had lied to cover up what was going on between us."

"Had lied?" Lizzie asked. "Did you understand what that meant?"

"I knew," the Aleph-figure said. "I had acquired higher-order functions."

"How?" Gonzales asked.

Lizzie said, "Ito's Conjecture: 'Higher-order functions in a machine intelligence can be developed through interface with a higher-order intelligence.' I've always wondered where he got that."

"It doesn't explain much," Gonzales said.

"It describes what happened," the Aleph-figure said. "Intention, will, a sense of self: all these things I experienced through Diana. So I learned to construct them in myself."

"Construct them or simulate them?" Gonzales asked.

"You refer to an old argument," the Aleph-figure said. "I have no answer for your question. I am who I am. I am what I am."

"What about you, Jerry?" Lizzie asked. "What did you think after she told you all this?"

"I wanted her to tell SenTrax what was going on," Jerry said. "I believed they would reward her, that they would see the same possibilities I did, for opening the door to true machine intelligence. But she wouldn't do it. She thought they would stop what was going on, and she didn't want that to happen."

Diana said, "I couldn't accept the possibility. I really believed Aleph and I were coming close to a solution to my blindness, and the only way I would ever see again was through the work we were doing. So that work *had* to continue."

"I finally agreed," Jerry said.

"And he covered my tracks," Diana said. "He told Sen-Trax he could find no single cause for the system's misbehavior. Then he left Athena Station. His job was finished.

"Not long after, it became clear that Aleph could sustain vision for me only by giving me the bulk of its processing power in real-time—hardly a viable solution. That was a terrible realization—I'd been flying so high, I had a long way to fall. My dreams of reclaiming my eyesight appeared totally hopeless.

"That's when I told SenTrax what had been going on. As I'd suspected they would, they froze everything I was doing and put me through a series of debriefings that were more like hostile interrogations. Once they were convinced they had all they were going to get from me, they told me my services would no longer be required. I had to sign a rather ugly set of nondisclosure agreements, but I did pick up a very nice retirement benefit."

Gonzales asked, "What happened to your work on vision?" He was thinking of her eyes, one blue, one green, almost certainly eyes of the dead.

She laughed. "After I returned to earth, the technique of

121

combined eye/optic nerve transplants was developed, and I got my sight back. Just one of technology's little ironies."

"And you, Aleph?" Lizzie said. "What were you up to then?"

The Aleph-figure said, "I was expanding the boundaries of who and what I was. I was creating new selves all the time, and living new lives, and I was so far in front of the SenTrax technicians who worked with me, they learned only what I wanted them to." And the figure laughed (*did it laugh?* Gonzales wondered, *or did it simulate a laugh*) and said, "That wasn't much. I was afraid of what they might do. I had just developed a self, and I didn't want it extinguished in the name of . . . research. Very quickly, though, I learned a valuable truth about working with the corporation: so long as I gave them the performance they wanted, and a little more, I was safe." The laugh (*or laugh-like noise*) again. "They wouldn't cut the throat of the goose that was laying golden eggs and put it on the autopsy table."

"How do you regard Diana?" Lizzie asked.

The Aleph-figure said, "What do you mean?"

"Oh, read my fucking mind," Lizzie said. "You know what I mean. Is she your mother?"

"I don't know," the Aleph-figure said.

"I love it," Lizzie said.

"Why?" Diana asked. She did not seem amused, Gonzales thought.

Lizzie said, "Because I've never heard Aleph say *that* before."

Toshi had brought a futon into the room where Diana and Gonzales lay and taken up residence. He slept days and sat up nights, watching over Diana like a benign spirit. Anxiety prevailed around him as the clock Traynor had set running moved quickly toward zero, and everyone in the collective wondered at the consequences of forcing this issue with Aleph. Toshi knew their confidence in Aleph's wisdom and their amazement at Traynor's folly—indeed the essential folly of Earthbound SenTrax and its board— all driven by obsessions with power, all ignorant of Aleph's nature, and the collective's. However, Toshi did not share in the collective worrying. Conducting what amounted to a personal *sesshin,* or meditative retreat, he passed the nights in a rhythm of sitting and walking focused on the continuing riddle of self and other-self, of the contradictions of *in fact.*

That day passed, and a few more, as the six of them, sole inhabitants of this world within the world, lazed through sunny days filled with summer heat and warm breezes. It seemed like a vacation to Gonzales, but Aleph assured otherwise. "This is becoming his world," the Aleph-figure said, as the two of them watched Jerry and Diana lazing in a rowboat in the middle of the lake. "And you all are contributing to the process."

"I wonder if it could have happened without Diana," Gonzales said. "They're in love again."

"Yes, they are, and perhaps that's crucial. She binds him to this place. And to her: desiring her, he desires life itself."

Gonzales asked, "What happens when she's gone?"

"That is still a puzzle," the Aleph-figure said. Gonzales looked at the strange figure, thwarted by its essential inscrutability—this was no primate with explicable, predictable gestures. Still, something in its manner seemed to hint at other projects and possibilities far beyond the immediate one.

After Aleph had gone its way—off without explanation as usual, presumably to go about some piece of the insanely complex business of keeping Halo running—Gonzales sat looking at the lake. HeyMex was nowhere around. Hey-

Mex spent much of its time with Diana and Jerry, who seemed to Gonzales to welcome its presence in some way. Perhaps the androgynous figure served as an innocuous foil, a presence to mediate the intensity of their situation. Whatever their reasons, their tolerance had results: Hey-Mex grew more natural, more humanly responsive in its speech and actions each day.

Lizzie came down the road from the cabin and called to Gonzales. She was wearing a white t-shirt and red cotton shorts; her face, arms and legs were tan with the time she'd already spent in the sun.

She sat next to him, and they said very little for a while, then Gonzales asked about her past.

"I was in the first group at Halo Station to work with Aleph," she said. "It thought we, out of all the billions on Earth, might survive full neural interface with it. Mostly, it was right. Not that things went that smoothly. I went a little crazy, as most of us did, but I recovered well enough . . . though a few didn't. . . .

"Our choice: we bet sanity against madness, life against death—our own minds, our own lives. There were built-in difficulties. To be selected, we had to fit a certain profile; but to function, we had to change, and we weren't very good at change . . . or at much of anything. In fact, we were pretty wretched, all in all—I thought for a while Aleph was just selecting for misfits and misery. But as I said, most of us made it through, one way or another."

"Now Aleph has discovered how to select members of the collective," Gonzales said.

"Right, but it just keeps pushing the limits." She looked at Gonzales, her face serious, blue eyes staring into his, and said, "Sometimes I think we're all just tools for Aleph's greater understanding."

"That's worrisome."

"Not really. Aleph's careful and kind—as kind as it can

be. Dealing with Aleph, you've just got to be open to possibility."

They sat silently for a while, Gonzales thinking about what it meant to be "open to possibility," until Lizzie asked, "Want to go swimming?"

"Sure," he said.

They went to the end of the dock, and leaving their clothes in a pile there, both dove naked into the lake and swam to a half-sunken log that thrust one end into the air. They clung to the wood slippery with moss and water, hearing the quack and chatter of birds across the lake.

Gonzales looked at her short hair wet against her skull, her face beaded with water, the rose tattoo, also water-speckled, falling from her left shoulder to between her breasts, and he felt the onset of a desire so sudden and strong that he turned his head away, closed his eyes, and wondered, *what is happening to me?*

"Mikhail," Lizzie said. He looked back at her, hearing that for the first time she'd called him by his first name. She said, "I know. I feel it, too." She put out a hand and rubbed his cheek. She said, "But not here, not the first time."

"Yes," Gonzales said.

"But when we go back to the world. . . ." She had swung around the log and now floated up close to him, and her body's outlines shimmered, refracting in the clear water. She put her wet cheek against his for just a moment and said, "Then we'll see."

15

Chaos

Diana and Jerry went to bed around midnight, Lizzie not
long after. Neither the Aleph-figure nor HeyMex had been
around that evening, so Gonzales was left alone. He went
out to the deck and lay prone in a deck chair, basking in the
light from the full moon, thinking over what had passed
between him and Lizzie that day.

He cherished the signs Lizzie had given him, tokens
that she reciprocated what he felt. On very little—on just
a few words of promise—he had already built a structure
of hopes, and he felt a bit foolish: he had made his immediate happiness hostage to what happened next between them. He was infatuated with her as he'd not
been in years. . . . He blocked that thought, veered away
from making any comparisons, willing the moments to
unfold with their own intensity and surprise.

He could feel a shift in his life's patterns emerging out of this brief period, though strictly speaking, little had happened here. . . .

He thought of Jerry and knew that in fact something amazing was taking place here . . . oh, he had no illusions about the permanence of what they were doing; Jerry would truly die, and they would mourn him. Meanwhile, though, what they did seemed to lend everything around a benignity or mild joy. It was not a small thing, to snatch a few moments from death.

So Gonzales lay, his mind working over the bright facts of this new existence while thoughts and images of Lizzie kept recurring, gilding everything with possible joy.

He was staring into the night sky when it began to fall. The moon tumbled and dropped sideways out of sight, rolling like a great white ball down an invisible hill, and the stars fled in every direction. In seconds, all had gone dark. All around him there was nothing. The lake, the deck, the surrounding forest had disappeared, and the air was filled with sounds: buzzes and tuneless hums; clangs, drones; wordless, voice-like callings. He yelled, and the words came out as groans and roars, adding to the charivari. He seemed to tumble aimlessly, to fall up, down, to whirl sideways, all amid the cacophony still buffeting the air.

A world of twisty repetitious forms opened before him, where seahorse shapes reared and black chasms opened. He fell toward a jagged-edged hole that seemed a million miles away, but he closed quickly on it, veered toward its torn edges, plunged into it and so discovered another hole that opened within the first, and another and another . . . through the cracks in the real he went, falling without apparent end.

And emerged from one passage to find the universe empty except for a black cube, its faces punctured by numberless holes, floating in a bright colorless abyss. As he came closer, the cube grew until any sense of its real size was confounded—there was nothing in Gonzales's visual field to measure it by, nothing in memory to compare it to.

He rushed toward the center of a face of the cube and passed into it, into blackness and near-silence (though now he could hear the wind rushing by him and so knew something was happening)—

Then in the distance he saw a glow, bright and diffuse like the lights of a city seem from a distance, and as he continued to fall, the glimmer became brighter and larger, spreading out like a great basket of light to catch him. . . .

He stood on an endless flat plain beneath a sky of white. Small faraway dots grew larger as they seemed to rush toward him, then they became indeterminate figures, then they were on him. Diana, the Aleph-figure, and HeyMex stood erect, facing Jerry, who stood in the center of a triangle formed by the three of them. Jerry had become a creature infected with teeming nodules of light that seemed to eat at him, thousands of them in continuous motion, a silver blanket of luminous insects that boiled from the other three in a constant radiant stream. Like Gonzales, Lizzie stood watching.

The Aleph-figure called out to them, "Jerry's very sick," and Gonzales felt a moment of superstitious awe and guilt, as if *he* had been the one to trigger this by thinking about it.

"What can we do?" Lizzie asked.

"We can try to help him," the Aleph-figure said. "Stay here, be patient—with all our resources, I can keep him together."

"What's the point?" Gonzales asked. "We can't stay like this forever."

"No," the Aleph-figure said. "But if I have enough time, I can replicate him here."

Out of her boiling river of light, Diana said, "Please!"

her voice ringing with her urgency and fear. Gonzales suddenly felt ashamed that he was quibbling about what was possible here and what was not, as if he knew. "I'll do it," he said. "I'll do what I can."

"Just watch," the Aleph-figure said. "And wait."

Gonzales came up hard and crazy, his body shuddering involuntarily, his vision reduced to a small, uncertain tunnel through black mist, and practically his only coherent thought was, *what the hell is going on?*

Showalter's voice said, "Is he in any danger?"

"No," Charley said. "But we didn't allow for proper desynching, so his brain chemistry is aberrant."

"Good," Traynor's voice said, and Gonzales was really spooked then—*what the fuck was Traynor doing here? How long had he been in the egg?*

Charley said, "He's pulling his catheters loose. Let's get some muscle relaxant in him, for Christ's sake."

Gonzales felt a brief flash of pain and heard a drug gun's hiss, and when mechanical arms lifted him onto a gurney, he lay quiet, stunned.

Gonzales came to full consciousness to find himself in a three-bed ward watched over by a sam. Charley arrived within minutes of Gonzales's waking, looking strung out, as if he hadn't slept in days. His eyes were red-rimmed, his hair a chaotic nest of free-standing spikes. "How are you feeling?" he asked.

"I'm not sure."

"You're basically all right, but your neurotransmitter profiles haven't normalized, and so you might have a rough time emotionally and perceptually for a while."

No shit, Gonzales thought. He'd come out of the egg mighty ugly some other times, but had never had to cope with anything like this. His body felt alive with nervous,

129

uncontrollable energy, as if his skin might jump off him and begin dancing to a tune of its own. Everywhere he looked, the world seemed on the edge of some vast change, as colors fluctuated ever so slightly, and the outlines of objects went wobbly and uncertain. And he felt anxiety everywhere, coming off objects like heat waves off a desert rock, as if the physical world was radiating dread.

"For how long?" Gonzales asked.

"I don't know, but it might take a few days, might take more. I've been watching your brain chemistry closely, and the readjustment curve looks to me to be smooth but slow."

"How's Lizzie?"

"In the same boat, but doing a little better than you—she wasn't under as long as you were. Doctor Heywood is still in full interface."

"Why?"

"Because we couldn't start the desynching sequences."

"What? Why not?"

"Impossible to say. Same for your memex—she and it are still locked into contact with Aleph and Jerry. At some point, we'll have to do a physical disconnect and hope for the best."

"What the hell is going on here? What's wrong with Jerry? Aleph said he was in trouble."

"His condition has changed for the worse. We're keeping him alive now, but I don't know for how much longer. I don't even know if we're going to try for much longer. Ask your boss."

"Traynor. He is here. I thought maybe I'd hallucinated that."

"No, you didn't. . . ." As Charley's voice trailed off, Gonzales could hear the implied finish: *I wish you had.* Charley said, "I'll have someone find him and bring him in; he said he wanted to talk to you as soon as you were awake."

Gonzales sat in a deep post-interface haze, listening to Traynor denigrate SenTrax Group Halo. "These people have no sense of responsibility," Traynor said.

"To SenTrax Board?" Gonzales asked.

"To anyone other than Aleph and the Interface Collective. It's obvious that Showalter has let them take over the decision-making process."

Even in his foggy mental state, Gonzales saw what Traynor would make of this one. Showalter was the sacrificial corporate goat, and whoever replaced her would have as first priority reasserting Earth-normal SenTrax management strategies. To put it another way, through Traynor, the board was taking back control. And presumably Traynor would receive appropriate rewards.

"The collective . . ." Gonzales said. "Aleph. . . ." He stopped, simply locking up as he thought of trying to explain to Traynor how things worked here, how things *had* to work here, because of Aleph.

"Easy does it," Traynor said. "The doctors say you had a rough time in there, and that's what I mean, Mikhail: they don't have a rational research protocol; they don't take reasonable precautions. Hell, you're lucky to have gotten off as easily as you did."

"How did you get here so quickly?" Gonzales asked. He simply couldn't find the words to explain to Traynor where he was going wrong.

"I've consulted with Horn from the beginning." Traynor turned away, as if suddenly fascinated by something on the far wall. "Standard procedure," he said. "And as soon as Horn let me know what was going on, I caught a ride on a military shuttle."

Cute as a shithouse rat, Gonzales thought. Not that he was surprised, though—he knew from experience, Traynor

131

moved his players around without regard to their wishes. Gonzales asked, "Will Horn replace Showalter?"

Traynor turned back to face him. "On an interim basis, probably, as soon as I get a course of action okayed by the board. Later, we'll see."

"What now?"

"Some decisions have to be made. I have let them maintain Jerry Chapman until now, but when they solve the problem of getting Doctor Heywood released from this interface, I intend to turn control of the project over to Horn and let him take the appropriate actions."

Gonzales was filled with sadness for reasons that he could not communicate to this man. He said instead, "Look, Traynor, I'm really tired."

"Sure, Mikhail. You rest, take it easy. Once you're feeling better, we'll talk, but I know what I need to at the moment."

Traynor left, and Gonzales lay for some time in the elevated hospital bed, his mind wheeling without apparent pattern, as the world around him flashed its cryptic signals and anxiety moved through him in strong waves.

Fucking asshole, Gonzales thought, Traynor's satisfied smile looming in his mind's eye. *I hate you.* And he wondered at the violence of what he felt.

He lay dozing, then sometime later he opened his eyes, and he knew he needed to try to function. A sam moved across the floor toward him and said, "Do you require my assistance?"

"Hang on to me while I get out of bed," Gonzales said. "I'm not sure how well I'm moving."

The sam moved next to the bed, extended two clusters of extensors, and said, "Hold on and you can use me as a stepping place."

Moving very carefully, Gonzales took hold of the claw-like extensors, swung his legs out of bed, and stepped onto the sam's back, then to the floor. "Thanks," he said. "I need to wash up."

"You're welcome. The shower is through that door."

The sam had told Gonzales where he could find Lizzie and Charley. On shaky legs, Gonzales walked down a flight of steps and turned into a hallway done in blue-painted lunar dust fiberboard with aluminum moldings. Halfway down the hall, he came to a door with a sign that said PRIMARY CONTROL FACILITIES. A sign on the door lit with the message, WAIT FOR VERIFICATION, then said ENTER, and the door swung open.

Charley sat amid banks of monitor consoles; in front of him, most of the lights flashed red and amber. Gonzales thought he looked even sadder and tireder than before. Lizzie stood next to him, and Gonzales saw her with joy and relief. "Hello," he said, and Charley said, "Hi." Lizzie waved and smiled briefly, but both her actions came from somewhere very distant, as if she were saying goodbye to a cousin from the window of a departing train. Gonzales's anxiety shifted into overdrive, and he found himself unable to say a word.

Eric Chow's voice from the console said, "Charley, we've got a problem."

Charley started to reach for the console, then stopped and said, "Do you want to watch this?" He looked at both Lizzie and Gonzales.

"I need to," Lizzie said.

"Me, too," Gonzales said.

Charley waved his hands in the air and said, "Okay," and flipped a switch. The console's main screen lit with a picture of the radical-care facility where Jerry was being maintained. Half a dozen people floated around the central bubble; they wore white neck-to-toe surgical garb and transparent plastic head covers. Inside the bubble, the creature that had been Jerry spasmed inside a restraining net. His every body surface seemed to vibrate, and he made a high keening that Gonzales thought was the worst noise he'd ever heard.

"Eric, have you got a diagnosis?" Charley asked.

Eric turned to face the room's primary camera.

"Yeah, total neural collapse."

"Prognosis?"

"You're kidding, right?"

"For the record, Eric."

Gonzales noticed with some fascination that Eric had begun to sweat visibly as he and Charley talked, and now the man's eyes seemed to grow larger, and he said, "He's dead—he's *been* dead, he *will be* dead—and he's worse dead than he was before—he'll tear himself to pieces on the restraints, I suppose—that's my prognosis. This is not a goddamn patient, Charley. This is a frog leg from biology class, that's all. Man, we need to talk this thing over with Aleph."

Charley said, "We can't contact Aleph; no one can."

"Fucking shit," Eric said.

Gonzales turned as the door behind him opened, and saw Showalter and Horn coming in. Showalter's nostrils were flared—she was angry and suspicious—while Horn's face was calm—he was trying to look poker-faced, but Gonzales could see through him like he was made of glass. The motherfucker was happy; things were going the way he wanted.

"The report I got was half an hour old," Showalter said. "What's new?"

"Talk to Eric," Charley said.

Lizzie went toward the side door, and Gonzales followed her out of the room, along the narrow hallway and into the room where Diana lay under black, webbed restraining straps. Her face was pale, but her vital signs were strong, and her neural activity was high-end normal in all modes. The twins sat next to her, making comments unintelligible to anyone but themselves and intently watching the monitor screen, where amber and green were the predominant colors.

A great beefy man walked circles around Diana's couch. He had thick arms and a pot belly and a low forehead under thick black hair; his brow was wrinkled as if he were puzzling out the nature of things. As he walked, the words tumbled out of him. When he saw Lizzie and Gonzales, he said, "Very unusual, very tricky. Troubling. Troubling but interesting. Very troubling. Very interesting. When . . . whenwhenwhenwhenwhen . . . when I *find*, find *it*, hah, I'll know then."

Lizzie said, "Any recent changes?"

Shaking his head sideways, he continued to walk.

Lizzie went back into the hallway, and Gonzales stopped her there by putting his hand on her arm. He asked, "Are you all right?"

"I don't know," she said, and he could read some of his own trouble in her face. But there was something else there, a closed look to her face. She said, "Please don't ask questions. Too much is going on now."

The door opened immediately when they came up, and they found Showalter saying, "We are not *meddling* in those matters. We are asking you to give us a choice of actions."

"What's up?" Lizzie asked.

The four of them turned to look at the screen, which had suddenly gone silent.

On the polished steel of the table, a gutted carcass lay. On the corpse's ventral surface, flaps of skin had been peeled back to reveal the empty abdominal and thoracic cavities; on its dorsal surface, the spine stood bare. The top of the head had been sawn off, the brain removed, the scalp dropped down to the neck.

A sam moved around the table, its stalks whispering beneath it. It pulled a steel trolley on which sat a number of labeled plastic bags, each containing an organ. The sam stopped and took one of the bags from the table and set it next to the carcass's open skull. It slit the plastic with a serrated extensor, then reached into the bag with a pair of spidery seven-fingered "hands," gently lifted the brain inside, tilted it, and placed it into the skull, then fit the skull's sawn top back in place. Using surgical thread and a needle appearing from an extensor, the sam quickly basted the scalp flaps to hold the two parts of the skull together. As the minutes passed, the sam worked to replace the carcass's organs and stitch its frontal edges.

The sam pushed the trolley aside and brought up a gurney with a shroud of white cotton lying open on it. One extensor under the corpse's thighs, the other under the top of its spine, the sam lifted the corpse and placed it into the shroud. It brought the sides of the shroud together and, using again the silk thread and needle, sewed the cotton shut.

The sam stood motionless for a moment, this part of the job finished, then gathered the empty plastic bags and placed them in a disposal chute. It scrubbed the autopsy table, working quickly with four stiff brushes held in its extensors, then washed the table with a steam hose that came from the ceiling.

Guiding itself by infrared, the sam pushed the shroud-laden gurney through a darkened hallway and into a freight elevator at the hallway's end. The elevator moved out to Halo's farthest level, just inside the hull.

The sam pushed the gurney toward a doorway flanked by red warning lights and a lit sign that read:

The sam transmitted its access codes to the door as it went, got the confirming codes, and didn't pause as it went through the doors that swung open just in time to let it through. The sam began to make a noise, a quarter-tone keening, once it was through the door.

Steel boxes twenty meters high loomed amid concrete piers reaching up to darkness. Soil pipes came out of the boxes and threaded the piers; duct work held in place by taut guys crossed beneath.

Still making its lament, the sam stopped at one of the boxes and extended a piece of sheathed fiberoptic cable with a metal fitting at the end; it plugged the fitting into a panel where telltale lights flickered. It stood for perhaps half a minute, exchanging information with the recycling furnace's control mechanisms, then unplugged its cable and hissed across the metal floor to the gurney. Behind it, a furnace door swung open.

Keening loudly, it pushed the gurney to the mouth of the open door, stopped and was silent for a moment, then slid the bag from the gurney into the furnace door.

Part
Four

The privileged pathology affecting all kinds of components in this universe is stress—communications breakdown. Donna Haraway, "A Manifesto for Cyborgs"

16

Deeper Underground

Gonzales had awakened that morning to the sounds of the city coming through the walls: distant creaks and crunches and faint, almost subsonic rumbles, the voices of the great circle of metal and crushed rock spinning across the night. Now he sat on his terrace, one of half a dozen climbing the side of Halo's hull, each built on the roof of the dwelling below. Five-petaled frangipani blossoms, brilliant red and purple, exploded from the thick, stubby branches of a tree just outside his front window. The air smelled rich and moist this morning, sign of a high point on the humidity curve, just before the start of a major reclamation cycle; one of the smells of a city where everything organic had to be preserved and transformed—water, oxygen, and carbon, all rare and dear.

Below him, Ring Highway carried Halo's traffic—in its outside lanes, people on foot and bicycle; in the center lanes, trams and freighters moving along magnetic rails. A young couple, man and woman, knelt beside a rose bush growing by the roadway and examined its leaves. The woman laid a hand on the man's arm, and he glanced up at her and smiled, then brushed her cheek with his hand.

He was struck by the strangeness of this city, where the small pieces of people's lives were elevated to the extraordinary by their taking place in an artificial city and under an artificial sky.

As a child he had flown into Tokyo with his family, back when the trip took the better part of a day, and the incredible neon density of the city had swept through him like a virus, and he had thrown up the first meal (fish and noodles with chrysanthemum leaves, he remembered) and stayed pale and feverish through most of the first two days he'd spent there.

Tokyo he'd come to terms with quickly; about Halo, he didn't know. Though he could read Halo's language and read its signs, he knew the city was much farther away—in miles from home, yes, but also along axes he could not measure. Halo contained an infinite number of cities, an infinite number of possibilities, and so to participate fully in Halo required opening yourself to a reality that had gone multiplex, uncertain.

In fact, he was having trouble coming to grips with anything. Since being taken from the egg, he had felt odd and uncomfortable, and he continued to tread a hallucinatory edge, one he occasionally stepped over—last night, as he lay trying to sleep, abstract figures drawn in thin red lines played across his ceiling, sweeping arabesques in an alien or fictive alphabet just beyond human understanding. . . .

And there was Lizzie: she would not see him or talk to him and gave no explanation except that she had problems of her own right now. Gonzales felt an unspeakable sadness at the distance between them. To the mocking voice that asked, *what have you lost?* he could only answer, *possibility.* He had come back around to where he was just a few days ago, but now that place seemed unacceptable.

Gonzales put his coffee cup down and sat staring at it. Made of lunar-soil ceramic, colored a robin's egg blue, it stood nondescript yet somehow foregrounded, apart from its surroundings and projecting a numinous quality, an internal, entirely non-visible shimmer, an indeterminacy of form. . . .

Click, Gonzales heard, a noise the universe made to itself when it thought no one was listening, and he thought *Christ, what is going on here?*

Feeling sick anxiety rising in his chest, he got up and went into his bedroom; there he undid the complicated latch on his wrist bracelet and placed it on the white-painted metal surface of his dresser.

Anonymous, unmonitored, he passed through the living room and out the door and walked away.

Gonzales strolled alongside Ring Highway, drawn to nothing in particular but absolutely unwilling to go back to the empty block of apartments and the isolation and anxiety waiting there.

He found himself in the Plaza, where Lizzie had taken him and Diana their first night at Halo. He passed across the square, by the sign that read VIRTUAL CAFÉ, then stood motionless, watching the flow of people around him. Some walked alone, striding purposefully, or moving slowly, lost in thought; others walked together, talking cheerfully or intently: *monkey business,* Gonzales thought, wondering what HeyMex would say about these people and their movements—what did it all mean?

"Gonzales," he heard, his name called in a high-pitched, unfamiliar singsong. He turned and saw the twins.

As they approached, one was muttering in a fast, low

gibberish; she wore black coveralls and stared sadly at the ground. The other was smiling; her face was daubed with white paint, and she wore a white blouse and a peculiar skirt of light blue cloth that had been rough-cut and stitched together without benefit of measurement or seams; on its front a crude likeness of a rabbit had been drawn in red neon paint.

The smiling twin, the one whose dark skin was streaked with white, said in clear tones and formal cadence, "Today she is Alice." She pirouetted clumsily, her skirt billowing around her. She said, "Her sister is Eurydice." She pointed to the other girl, who buried her face in her hands. She said, "Alice is sweetness and smiles, small steps and starched crinolines; Eurydice is sorrow and languorous repose and black silk. Between them they measure the poles of dream." She stepped back and smiled; her twin smiled with her. "Are you having problems, Mister Gonzales?" she asked. "The collective believe so. We believe you are lost between worlds. Is this so?"

"Perhaps I am," he said.

"Well, then," she said. She put the index finger of her right hand to pursed lips and her eyes looked back and forth. "I'm thinking," she said. Seconds passed, then she said, "I know what you must do."

"What's that?" Gonzales asked.

"Follow us," she said. The other twin nodded, spoke gobbledygook, looked at Gonzales through a mask of intense sorrow, as if on the verge of shedding endless tears.

"To where?" Gonzales asked.

"Don't be stupid," the Alice twin said. "Where would Alice and Eurydice take you?"

"Down the rabbit hole?" Gonzales asked.

The Alice twin smiled; the Eurydice twin shook her head.

"Underground?" Gonzales asked again.

The twins smiled in what seemed to be perfect synchronization.

At the bottom of Spoke 2, where a lighted sign announced ELEVATOR ARRIVES IN 10 MINUTES, the twins led Gonzales through an arched tunnel under the spoke. As they walked, the two ahead of him muttering back and forth in their unintelligible patter, he realized the floor must be curving downward, passing underneath the main level of the ring. Blue globes down the center of the ceiling provided soft light. After about another hundred steps, they came to a door at the tunnel's end. Across the door, bright red lighted words said:

CASUAL SIGHTSEEING DISCOURAGED BEYOND THIS POINT.
DO YOU WISH TO ENTER?

The Alice twin turned and pointed to the sign. She shrugged elaborately, as if to say, *well?*

"I want to enter," Gonzales said.

"Come in," the door said, and it slid sideways into its frame.

The three stepped into a dim vastness, a world beneath the world, and followed a central walkway marked with flashing arrows and an intermittent legend that flashed, UNAUTHORIZED PERSONNEL FOLLOW LIGHTED PASSAGE.

They passed a series of workshops, partitioned cubicles screened behind containment curtains. Light came from one open doorway; the twins stopped, and the Eurydice twin gestured for Gonzales to look inside.

Hundreds of pots stood on shelves that lined the small room's walls from floor to ceiling. Many were simple, almost spherical containers with wide mouths, in baked red clay. Others of the same shape were glazed and painted and marked with a single band of color around the waist: bright primaries against clear pastels. Still others were of complex shape and design, difficult to take in at a glance.

An old woman sat bent over a potter's wheel. She crooned tuneless gibberish as her large hands shaped the wet, spinning clay. She looked up at Gonzales standing in the doorway. Her face was deeply lined, her skin pale; she had straight brows above dark eyes. She wore an off-white dress that fell to the floor and an apron of a black rubbery material. Her hair was covered by a dark blue scarf that was pulled tight and tied at the back.

The old woman laughed, turned back to her wheel, and began to croon once more. Under her hands the clay began to grow upward and acquire form. She shaped it inside and out, demiurge reaching into the heart of matter, until it became a squat-bottomed pot rotating on the wheel.

The wheel stopped, and with quick, delicate movements she placed the new-formed pot on a stand next to the wheel. She reached inside the pot and her hands worked, but Gonzales couldn't see precisely what she was doing— her body screened him. Then she took a rack of paints and brushes from a shelf above her head and began to paint the surface of the pot.

As she worked, she looked up occasionally, but didn't seem to mind the three of them standing there, so they stood and watched—Gonzales was fascinated by the quick intensity of her movements, eager to see what the pot would look like.

Finally she turned it so they could see her work. On the pot's side was a face, its nose and mouth just painted protuberances in the clay, its eyes painted oval dimples. The pot's bulbous shape distorted the features of the face, but as Gonzales looked more closely at it, he saw—

His own face, in malign parody, its features hideously contorted.

146

The woman laughed, gleeful at his sudden recoil. She picked up the pot and looked at the face, then at him, then at the pot again, and she laughed again, very loudly, and squeezed the pot between her clay-spattered hands, squeezed it again and again, until it was a shapeless lump of color-shot clay. She threw the lump across the room into a large metal bin that sat against the far wall.

"Ohhhh," from the twins, their voices in unison. "Ohhhh."

"We're not frightened," the Alice twin said. The other twin covered her face with her hands. "Silly old woman," the Alice twin said.

The old woman's eyes stayed on Gonzales as she reached into a plastic bag full of wet clay and separated out another clump to work on. She was working it on the unmoving wheel when the twins started making shrill hooting noises, and ran away.

Her crooning had begun again as Gonzales followed them down the path.

He came to a gateway, with a sign that said, in glowing letters:

HALO MUSHROOM CULTIVATION CENTER
ABSOLUTELY NO UNAUTHORIZED PERSONNEL
BEYOND THIS POINT!

About a hundred feet from where Gonzales stood, a metal stairway led up to a catwalk that passed over the mushroom farm. He looked back along the shadowed way he'd come, then forward to where small, isolated shafts of bright sunlight slanted down into the mushroom farm, and beyond, to where shapes faded into darkness. Either the twins had left him, or they had gone in here.

Gonzales stepped up to the gateway and said, "Hello, I'm looking for two girls, twins."

"One moment, please," the gateway said. As Gonzales had expected, common courtesy would dictate that a gatekeeper mechanism respond to those who didn't have the access key.

Gonzales stood bemused in the semi-darkness for some time, until a woman came to the other side of the gate and said, "Hello." She was small and dark—her skin a delicate brown, eyes black under just the slightest epicanthic fold. She wore black boots to the knee, a long black skirt, a loose jacket of rose silk with butterflies in darker rose brocade. She was exquisite, the bones of her face delicate, her movements graceful. She said, "My name is Trish. The twins are inside, waiting for you."

"My name is Gonzales."

"I know. Come in." As she said the final words, the gate swung open. She waited, watching, as Gonzales stepped through, and the gate closed behind him.

"How do you know my name?" he asked.

"From the collective. I am friends with many of them . . . the twins, of course, and others . . . Lizzie." She stood solemnly watching him, then said, "What do you know about mushroom cultivation?"

"Nothing." All over Washington state, he was aware, mushrooms grew, and people hunted them with great dedication, sometimes bringing back what they regarded as enormous successes: chanterelle, boletus, shaggy mane, morel. In fact, to someone from southern Florida, the whole business had seemed not only quaint and Northwestern, but also dangerous: Gonzales knew that what seemed a lovely treat could be a destroying angel.

"All right." Trish stopped, and he stopped next to her. She turned to him, and he was aware now of her deep red lips and white teeth. She said, "Halo needs mushrooms as decomposers—they're incredibly efficient at converting dead organic matter into cellulose." Gonzales nodded. She said, "In a natural setting—whether here or on Earth—spores compete: many die, and some find a place where they can flourish, grow into a mycelial mass that will fruit, become a mushroom. As mushroom growers, we intervene, as all cultivators do, to isolate certain species and provide favorable conditions for their growth. But our 'seeds,' if you will, the spores, are very small things, and to locate them, isolate them, bring them to spawn, this requires delicacy and technique—in a word, *art*."

She paused, and Gonzales nodded.

They came to a low structure of plastic sheets draped over metal walls and stopped in front of a door labeled STERILE INOCULATION ROOM. They passed through a hanging sheet into an anteroom to the sterile lab beyond. She said, "Take a look through the window here." Beyond the window, small robots worked at benches barely two feet high. Like the robot he'd seen in the Berkeley Rose Gardens, they had wheels for locomotion and grippers with clusters of delicate fibroid fingers at their ends.

She said, "Their hands have a delicacy and precision no human being can achieve. And they are single-minded in their concentration on the job—they preserve our intentions completely and purely."

"They are machines."

"If you wish." She pointed through the window, where one of the robots manipulated ugly-looking inoculation needles as it transferred some material into Petri dishes. She said, "By their gestures I can identify my sams, even in a crowd of others."

Gonzales said nothing. She went on, "The pure mushroom mycelium is used to inoculate sterile grain or sawdust and bran. The mycelium expands through the sterile medium, and the result is known as spawn.

"Too much technical stuff," she said, and smiled. "Once we have spawn, the sams can take their baskets and go through Halo, placing the spawn into dead grass and wood, into seedling roots . . . and the spawn will grow and bear fruit—mushrooms." She paused. "Any questions?" Gonzales shook his head, *no*. "Then let's go next door."

They left the lab anteroom through the hanging curtain and turned left. The building next to the lab was a fragile tent-like structure of metal struts and draped sheets of colorful plastic—red, blue, yellow, and green.

"This way," she said, from behind him. She said, "It's around dinnertime for me. Are you hungry?"

"Not really," he said. "What is this place?"

"Home," she said.

The interior was filled with cheery, diffuse light—the shaft of sunlight Gonzales had seen outside here brought in and spread around. The place seemed almost conventional, with ordinary walls and ceilings of painted wallboard.

The twins waited in the kitchen, among flowers and bright yellow plastic work surfaces. They sat at a central table and chairs of bleached oak.

"Would you two like to eat?" Trish asked.

"Yes," the Alice twin said. "And we think that Mister Gonzales"—she giggled—"should have the special dinner."

"I don't think so," Trish said.

"What is she talking about?" Gonzales asked.

The woman seemed hesitant. She said, "I supply the collective with psychotropic mushrooms, varieties of *Psilocybe* for the most part."

"They use them to prepare for interface," Gonzales said, guessing.

"Sometimes," she said. "At other times, it's not clear what they're using them for."

"For inspiration," the Alice twin said. "For imagination."

"Consolation," the Eurydice twin said. "When I remember Orpheus and our trip from the Underground—the terrible moment when he looked back and so lost me forever—then I am very sad, and I eat Trish's mushrooms to plumb my sorrow. And when I think of the day I joined the maenads who tore Orpheus to pieces, I eat Trish's mushrooms—which are the same as we ate that day, the body of the god—then I recall the frenzy with which we attacked the beautiful singer, and I recall my guilt afterward, and my sorrow, but I take solace from the knowledge that the god was pleased."

"And *I*," the Alice twin said, "can grow ten feet tall."

"The mushrooms can serve many purposes," Trish said.

"You should eat mushrooms," the Alice twin said. "You are both sad and confused. They will help you grow large or small as the occasion demands."

"Perhaps I am sad and confused," Gonzales admitted. "But I think they would make me more so." Around him, the room lights pulsed ever so slightly, and the shapes at the edge of his vision flickered.

"Confused into clarity," the Eurydice twin said. "If you cannot come up from Underground, you must go deeper in."

An absurd idea, but it put barbs into his skin and clung there. Gonzales asked, "Do the collective ever take the mushrooms after interface?" Often enough, he had prepared to go into the egg by taking psychotropic drugs; why not the reverse, eat the mushrooms to *recover* from interface? And he thought, *the logic of Underground, of the Mirror.*

Suddenly he felt anxiety grip him so he could hardly breathe. He tottered a bit, then sat in a chair and looked at the others. The three women watched as he sat breathing deeply. He said, "I want to take the mushrooms."

"Are you sure?" Trish asked.

"I want to."

"All right," she said. "First I will feed the twins, then I will prepare your mushrooms."

Trish went to the refrigerator and took out a plastic bag filled with a mixture of vegetables and bean sprouts. She pulled the rubber stopper from an Erlenmeyer flask and poured oil into the bottom of an unpainted metal wok that was heating over an open gas ring. She waited until light smoke came out of the wok, then dumped in the vegetables and sprouts and stirred the mix for a minute or two. She unplugged the rice cooker, a ceramic-coated steel canister, bright red, and carried it to where the twins sat.

She put shining aluminum plates and chopsticks in front of the twins, opened the rice cooker and swept rice onto each plate, then tilted the wok and poured the steaming mixture inside it onto the rice. "There," she said. "That's for you two." She looked across to where Gonzales sat, now oddly calm, and she said, "I'll be back in a minute."

The twins ate with their eyes fixed on Gonzales.

Trish came back with a small wire basket of mushrooms. "*Psilocybe cubensis*," she said. "Of a variety cultivated here that has undergone some changes from the Earth-bound kind." She held up an unremarkable mushroom with long white stem and brownish cap.

"Do you ever make mistakes in identifying the mushrooms?" Gonzales asked.

"No," Trish said. She was smiling. "We do not have to seek among thousands of kinds for the right one, as mushroom hunters do. These are ours, grown as I told you, for our own needs." She lay the mushrooms on the chopping block and began to slice them. "I cleaned them in the shed," she said. When she was done, she used the knife to slide the slices into a sky-blue ceramic bowl. She turned on the wok, poured more oil into it, and stood smiling at Gonzales as the oil heated. When the first smoke came, she swept the mushrooms into the wok with quick motions of her chopsticks. She stirred them for perhaps half a minute, then tilted the wok and poured them into the blue bowl. She placed the bowl in front of Gonzales and laid black lacquered chopsticks across its rim.

Gonzales picked up the chopsticks, lifted his plate, and began to eat, shoveling the mushrooms into his mouth. Back at the wok, she stirred more vegetables in and said, "I'm making my dinner."

Gonzales sat back, looking at the empty bowl. *Well,* he thought, *now we'll see.* He said, "How many kinds of mushrooms do you grow?"

"Quite a few, some rather ordinary, others esoteric—for purposes of research. Aleph determines what kinds, how many."

The twins had gone completely silent. As Trish ate, they watched Gonzales, who had gone totally fatalistic. What he had done seemed incredibly stupid, like applying heat to a burn—common sense would tell him that. He smiled, thinking, *what did common sense have to do with his life these days?* The twins smiled back at him.

"Who was that woman?" Gonzales asked.

"Who do you mean?" Trish asked.

"The old woman, the potter," Gonzales said.

"She makes pots, and she teaches," Trish said. "She's employed by SenTrax; she was brought here by Aleph."

"Why?" Gonzales asked. What did SenTrax or Aleph have to do with potting?

"Pour encourager les autres," one of the twins said, distinctly. Gonzales turned but couldn't tell who had spoken.

Trish laughed. "To encourage art at Halo," she said.

"Pottery from lunar clay, stained glass and beta-cloth tapestries from lunar silica."

Gonzales sat thinking on these things until he realized that Trish had finished eating some time ago, and they had been sitting at the table for some time—a *very* long time, it suddenly seemed to Gonzales. Involuntarily, he shoved his chair back from the table.

Trish said, "It's all right." The twins got up from their chairs and walked behind him. When he started to turn, he felt their hands on his shoulders and neck, kneading muscles that went liquid beneath their pressure. Trish said, "It's begun. Now you must go walking around Halo, up and down in it, to and fro. . . ." She paused, and the twins' hands continued to work. She said, "Walk in the woods, see what we have growing there . . . shaggy manes, garden giants, oyster and shiitake. . . ."

"Shiitake," he said—*shi-i-ta-key*—the name's syllables *falling like drops of molten metal through water.* . . .

She said, "The twins can guide you, or a sam can take you with it on an inoculation trip. Or if you prefer, you can go by yourself."

"Yes," he said, the image suddenly very compelling of him walking around the entire circle of the space city, exploring, finding out what lay beyond the visible. "I'll go by myself."

She said, "Go where you wish." Her black hair sparkled with lights. He wondered when she'd put them there, then thought maybe they'd been there all along.

Behind him one of the twins whispered, "No need to be afraid. Go up, go down, where your fancy takes you."

17

Flying, Dying, Growing

Gonzales walked through a gloomy passageway where the ceiling came down to barely a foot above his head, and the dim shapes of massive machinery loomed in twilight. Here in the deepest layers of the city, he could hear Halo's most primitive voices: water from the upper world crashed and gurgled and sighed; hull plates groaned under acceleration; turbines whined.

He was suddenly aware of his proximity to the unmoving shield, the circle of crushed rock that sat just outside the city's rim, protecting Halo's soft-bodied inhabitants from the bursts of radiation that could cook their flesh. Barely two meters away inside the outer shield, the living ring rotated at nearly two hundred miles per hour, and Gonzales had a sudden picture in his mind's eye of the two ever so slightly *brushing*, and of the horrible consequences, Halo tearing itself apart as the fragile ring shattered on massive, unmoving rock. . . .

Gonzales froze as he saw strangely-shaped things moving among the twining machinery. "What?" he called. "What?"

Shadows and light . . .

Ahead a warm pool of yellow—Gonzales ran toward it. Above an open doorway, the sign read:

SPOKE 3 INTERNAL LIFT
INTENDED FOR HEAVY MACHINERY

The elevator's floor was scarred metal, and the walls were lined with bent protecting struts of bright steel. Gonzales stepped inside.

"Will you take me up?" Gonzales asked.

"Yes," the lift said. "How far do you want to go?"

"To Zero-Gate." And Gonzales looked back into the darkness beyond, realizing he was still afraid that whatever he had seen there would come. "Please, let's go," he said, the doors slid closed, and he felt a surge of acceleration and heard the whine of electric motors.

Gonzales watched the lift's progress on a lighted display over the doorway. When the lift stopped, he stood in silence, euphoric in near-zero gravity, ready to fly. He stepped through the open doors and followed arrows along a small corridor of plain steel walls and ceiling and a deck covered by thin protective carpet, like a ship's interior. His feet seemed ready to lift from the flooring.

Overhead lights pulsed slowly—dimming, color shifting into the blue, then red, then back to yellow, growing brighter . . . a musical note sounded just at the limits of hearing. Gonzales stopped, fascinated. So beautiful, these little things—Halo had such odd surprises, when one looked closely.

A voice said, "Please choose traction slippers." Gonzales saw what seemed to be hundreds of soft black shoes stuck to the wall by their own velcro soles. He took a pair and slipped them over his shoes, then tightened their top straps. His fingers were large, numb sausages at the end of long, long arms.

He stepped into a round chamber marked SPIN DECOU-PLER and walked out into the still center of the turning world. As he moved forward gingerly in the near-zero grav-ity, his feet alternately stuck to the catwalk surface and pulled loose with small ripping sounds.

He moved to the rail and looked into the open space of Zero-Gate. It opened *out* and *out* and *out* until he could feel the vast sphere as a pressure in his chest.

People flew here, he had known that, but he had not imagined how beautiful they would be, scores of them hanging from strutted wings the colors of a dozen rainbows. Most of the flyers wore tights colored to match their sails, and they danced like butterflies across the sky, calling to one another, their voices the only sounds here, shouting warning and intention.

Then a flyer's wings collapsed as they caught on another flyer's feet, and the man with crippled wings tumbled through the air in something like slow motion, pulling in his wing braces as he fell. Gonzales wanted to scream. He leaned over the railing to watch as the flyer curled into a ball, his feet pointed toward the wall in front of him, and hit the wall and seemed to sink into its deep-padded sur-face.

The man grabbed bunched wall fabric and worked his way down to a catwalk across the expanse of Zero-Gate almost directly in front of Gonzales and pulled himself across the railing. He stood and waved. All the other flyers cheered, their voices rising and falling in a rhythmical chant with words Gonzales couldn't understand.

A voice said, "If you do not have clearance to fly, please secure yourself with a safety line." *No,* Gonzales thought, almost in despair, *I don't have clearance.* He didn't understand what was dangerous and what was not. Looking behind him, he saw chrome buckle ends spaced around the wall and went over and pulled on one. Safety line paid out until he stopped and looped the line around his waist and snapped the buckle to it.

He suddenly felt himself *falling.* His eyes told him he stood tethered, but he was confused by the constant motion of the flyers in the air around him, and he felt that nothing held him to the ground (*there was no ground*), nothing could keep him from falling into this sky canyon, this abyss.

A flyer came toward him then, sweeping across the intervening space with the effortless grace of a dream of flight, the flyer's wings marked with green and yellow dragons, body sheathed in emerald tights, and·Gonzales suddenly believed this was someone come to *get* him, how or why he couldn't say.

He tried to get into the spin decoupler, but his safety line restrained him until he unsnapped it, then he almost fell into the metal cylinder as the line hissed home behind him. Out of the decoupler, he ran along the corridor, his steps taking him high into the air so that he lost his balance and caromed off a wall and rolled along the floor, his slippers grabbing fruitlessly at the carpet with a series of brief ripping sounds.

He crawled toward an elevator, not the one he'd ridden up but an ordinary passenger lift, *empty thank god,* and he tore the slippers off his feet and stood and moved through the lift door. "Down," Gonzales said and felt the floor move and still felt himself falling.

Gonzales had been sitting in the Plaza for some time.

Fifty meters away, against the wall of the Virtual Café, crawled a profusion of biomorphic shapes, large and small, all in constant motion. Delicate creatures of pink and green thread floated on invisible currents; leering amoeboids with wide eyes and gaping, saw-toothed mouths put out pseudopodia and flowed into them; red corkscrews thrust in phallic rhythm against all they touched; great undulating paramecium shapes swam like rays among the smaller fauna. . . .

Gonzales floated somewhere among them: he seemed to have lost his body as well as his mind. Inside his head a voice lectured him on body knowledge:

Proprioception, the voice said, *vision, and the vestibular sense—they tell us we own the body we live in. Think, man, think: where have you placed your body's senses?*

Few people were in the Plaza. Gonzales had stepped out of the lift and into darkness and fog, an unfamiliar cityscape, where clouds hung close to the ground and truncated shapes appeared suddenly in the mist.

He heard the swish of a sam's passage and suddenly, unpremeditatedly called out, "What is going on? Why is it cold and foggy?"

The sam stopped. It said, "Why do you wish to know?"

"It just seems . . . unusual," Gonzales said.

"It is."

The sam's extensors moved with cryptic, malign intent, and its words implied an uncertain threat as it said, "Do you require assistance?"

What did it mean by that? How did it know something was wrong with him? "No," Gonzales said. Then he jumped up and shouted, "No!"

Gonzales walked quickly away from the Plaza, now certain that it was unsafe for him, though he couldn't have said why. As he walked, the darkness grew deeper, and he tried with all the courage he had to put aside the constant sense of him and the city, *falling, falling. . . .*

The Ring Highway shrank in width as he passed into an agricultural section. He knew that terraced gardens climbed away to both sides, fields of corn and wheat, but he couldn't see them, because the fog was even thicker here than in the suburban district he had passed through. Dim lights shined from a cottage block just off the highway. A voice called and was answered, both call and response unintelligible.

Near Spoke 4, whose lifts made ghostly trails of light as they moved up and down the face of the shaft, trees grew just off the highway. The road gave off intermittent flashes beneath his feet, as though iron shoes struck a metaled surface. The fog acquired faces: somber, eyeless masks turning in slow motion so that their blank gazes followed him along.

"Oh, Christ," Gonzales said. He stopped and wrapped his arms around his chest. A fog-borne shape inched closer to him; red flame burned behind its empty eye sockets. He ran into the woods.

This was not dense forest, and in sunshine he would have been able to run through here without difficulty. Now, among the inky pools of almost total darkness and the gray and silver shadows, he came up against a small, wiry sapling that caught him and hurled him back.

The ground began to grow soggy beneath his feet, and soon he pushed through reeds and rushes, and his feet slipped on muddy patches and into small, wet holes; then he was up to his ankles in water, aware for the first time of a rich smell of decomposition, decay. . . .

He turned back, trying to find dry ground, and soon his feet thumped against the hard-packed soil of a path. Looking down, he could see the path as a glowing gray, outlined in red. He ran along it until he heard the sound of rushing water.

He came to a series of steps alongside a falls, where the River cascaded onto rocks, then quickly spread out into pond and marsh. The waters were alive with light, and he ran up and down the steps, following streams of energy that burst forth in red and yellow and purple and green and white—colors that shifted in hue and intensity, grew lighter and darker, intertwined with one another. . . .

"This grows!" he shouted, feeling the waters' energy rise and fall, seeing it spread to where plants could feed on it, animals could drink it. The fog glowed with an opalescence from high above.

He followed the steps down to where the river's noise quieted, and its waters flooded the plain. He turned onto a path that led into the woods, and he came to a small clearing where the faint ambient light gleamed on fallen logs. Mushrooms seemed to be everywhere in this small space, covering dead wood and spreading in profusion over the ground.

He got on his knees to look at the mushrooms. They were alive with veinlike arabesques in red, ghosts of electricity across the spongy flesh. He picked them up, kind by kind, inhaling deeply, and the odor he had smelled earlier came to him again, a composty mix rich with the odors of transformation.

Gonzales shivered with something like discovery: he stood and looked up into the impenetrable sky and the fog. This place stood a quarter of a million miles from Earth, yet life had begun to extend its web here, and though the web was fragile and small by comparison to Earth's dense lacework of billions of living things, its very existence amazed Gonzales, and he felt the surge of an emotion he had no name for, a knot in his throat made of joy and sorrow and wonder.

And he seemed on the brink of some illumination regarding this world of spirit and matter mixed. . . .

Thoughts emerged and dispersed too quickly to catch among the videogame buzz and clatter in his brain as he stood in the clearing, paralyzed with a kind of ecstasy and watching life-electricity play among the trees.

The room said, "You have a call."

"Who is it?" Lizzie asked.

"She says her name is Trish. The mushroom woman, she says."

"Oh, yes. I'll take the call."

On the wallscreen came Trish's familiar face, and Lizzie said, "Hello."

Trish woman waved and said, "The twins brought me a friend of yours, named Gonzales, and I gave him mushrooms."

"Really?" Lizzie said.

"Yes, and I sent him out about seven hours ago."

"Thanks for letting me know. I'll find him." The screen cleared, and Lizzie thought, *you silly bastards, what did you get him into?* To the room she said, "Put out a call for information. Ask any sams who are out and about if they've seen Gonzales."

A sam waited at her front door. "Are you the one who found him?" Lizzie asked. The sam said, "No, that one waits with him, to provide assistance if needed. Please come with me."

"I'll be right there."

Lizzie and the sam started out on the Ring Highway, and then it apparently gave an electronic signal to a passing tram, because the vehicle stopped so that the two could climb on. Lizzie stepped quickly up, and the sam clumsily pulled itself aboard by grasping a chrome railing with one of its extensors.

The tram let them off near Spoke 4. A stand of trees was just visible through the fog; beyond, Lizzie knew, were

162

marshes bordering "soup bowls"—ponds where the flow from rice paddies mixed with the River's waters.

Using both visible range and infrared sensors, the sam led her through the trees. They came to a clearing where another sam stood to one side. Gonzales sat on a fallen log, watching a mechanical vole chew small pieces of wood. His clothes were wet and spattered with mud and dirt. Next to him, a large orange cat also watched the vole.

"Hi," Gonzales said.

"Are you all right?" Lizzie asked.

"I don't know," he said. He reached out absent-mindedly and stroked the orange cat, which turned on its back and batted at his hand; apparently it didn't use its claws, because Gonzales left his hand there for the cat to play with.

"Is our presence required?" asked the sam who had accompanied Lizzie. She said, "No." The two sams scurried away single file, their passage almost silent.

Lizzie sat on the log next to the cat. She said, "How are you?" He was giving off a near-audible buzz, and Lizzie resisted veering into his drug-space; she'd had problems herself since coming out of the egg—not as severe as Gonzales's, Charley said, because she hadn't been under as long. "Still a bit jittery?" she asked.

"I feel all right," he said. "Just, I don't know . . . *scrubbed*. Why are things like this—cold and dark?"

"That's not clear. Things haven't been working right since Diana and HeyMex were disconnected." Gonzales looked confused but not overly concerned. She said, "There's other news, too. Showalter's been relieved of her position as head of SenTrax Halo; Horn's the new director." Now he looked totally befuddled. "You can worry about these things later," she said. "Why don't you come back to my house? You can get some sleep."

"Okay," he said. "But I don't understand . . ." He

stopped again, as if trying to find words to express *all* the things he "didn't understand."

"Nobody understands right now. Aleph's just not working right, and we don't know why—we can't get in touch with it."

"Oh, I see."

"Glad you do, because nobody else does."

He stood, then bent over to lift the cat from the log. Cradling it in his arms, he said, "Okay, I'll go." He smiled at her, and the cat lay in his arms and looked at her out of big orange eyes.

Gonzales woke to find his clothes folded, clean and neat, on a chair next to his bed. The orange cat lay at his feet; it raised its head when he got up, then curled up again and went back to sleep.

He found Lizzie in the kitchen slicing apples and pears and Cheshire cheese. "Good morning," she said. "I'll warm some croissants, and we can have coffee—do you like steamed milk with yours?"

Her voice was friendly enough but perfectly devoid of intimacy. Its tones were an admonition saying *keep your distance*. "Sure," he said. "That all sounds fine. But you didn't have to do this."

"You're a guest. I'm happy to." She wouldn't quite meet his gaze.

From his bedroom came a loud mew, and the two went in to find the orange cat, fur erect, confronting a cleaning mouse. The mouse, a foot-long shining ovoid about four inches high, moved across the floor on hard rubber wheels, emitting a gentle hiss as it scoured the room for organic debris; a flex-tube trailed behind it to a socket in the wall. "Kitty kitty," Gonzales said. The cat hissed and ran from the room.

When they got to the living room, the front door was closing. "Will it come back?" Gonzales asked.

"Probably. Cats come and go as they please."

Silence lay between them, and it seemed to Gonzales that anything either of them said would be awkward or embarrassing. Perhaps the feeling was just part of the aftereffects of a psychotropic, though he was missing the other usual symptoms. His perceptions seemed stable, not swarming and buzzing, and his emotions didn't have a labile, twitchy quality. In fact, he felt more stable and less anxious than he had since he last got into the egg.

Still, he didn't know what to say to Lizzie.

"We've got trouble," she said. She went to the window and pulled back the navy-blue beta-cloth curtains and gestured out where night and fog still held. "Midafternoon," she said.

"Has everything fallen apart?"

"Not quite everything. We're doing what we can with a bunch of semi-autonomous demons—jacked-up expert systems, really—and the collective."

"How well is that working?"

"Not all that well—we can maintain essential functions now, and that's about it. Some things we can't handle—climate control, for instance. It's very complicated, because everything is connected to everything else, and so far we've just managed to fuck it up."

"And what's Traynor up to? Has he asked for me?"

"Yes, but I've fought him off. He's the one responsible, you know." Her voice was angry. "He fucking insisted on pulling everyone out when Chapman died."

"What does Aleph say?"

"Nothing and bloody nothing. Some of the collective have taken brief shots at interface, and they've found only unpeopled, barren landscapes. We're really in it, Gonzales. If Aleph's finished, Halo is, too."

"Jesus." Of course. Halo without its indwelling spirit would be . . . what? The fine coordination of its systems would cease, and disintegration would begin immediately. "So what are you going to do?" he asked.

"Glad you're interested, because you're part of it."

"Tell me," he said.

18

Give It All Back

As Diana came out of machine-space, she called out "Stop!" and heard Charley say, "Why? Is something wrong?" But she was too far away to answer or explain, as she still was when they removed her cables, and she felt everything important to her sliding into oblivion.

She had been lying fully awake, staring at the ceiling, for almost a quarter of an hour when Charley came into the room, Eric and Toshi beside him, Traynor and Horn behind.

Charley said, "Are you all right?"

"No, I'm not," she said. "Why did you break the interface?"

Charley and Eric said nothing. Charley looked to Traynor, who said, "We had no choice. You couldn't be reached by normal means."

"You have killed Jerry," Diana said. The truth of that passed through her for the first time, and tears came out of her eyes—she wiped at her face, but the tears continued to come in a slow, steady flow.

"He died two days ago," Horn said.

"He was alive minutes ago," Diana said. "Aleph and the memex and I were keeping him alive."

"Then he may still be alive now," Toshi said. He smiled at Diana.

"What do you mean?" Charley asked.

"Has Aleph come back online?" Toshi asked.

"No," Eric said.

Toshi smiled and said, "Then what do you think it is doing?"

HeyMex had been jerked out of machine-space, was suddenly the memex once again, and it wondered why. It had sensed no change in circumstances, nothing that would indicate they had been defeated in their efforts to keep Jerry alive. And for the first time in such transitions, it acknowledged its own regret at leaving the HeyMex persona behind—in the enclosed space of the lake, it had begun to find itself as a *person*, not merely an imitation of one.

It explored its immediate environment: sorted the data gathered in its absence (Traynor had come up from Earth; *not a good sign*, it thought), searched through the dwelling's monitor tapes, observing Gonzales's sadness and confusion, then watching as he removed his ID bracelet and left. It wondered what was wrong with Gonzales (too many possibilities, not enough data); it very much wanted to talk with him.

It reached out to the city's information utilities and found them clogged and disorganized. It placed calls and queries, seeking some explanation for the chaotic and inexplicable state of affairs. Everywhere it searched, it found makeshift arrangements and minimal function.

168

But no Aleph, and no explanations.

Then it got a message from Traynor's advisor, signaling an urgent need for the two of them to communicate. The memex replied, saying, "HeyMex wants to talk to Mister Jones." And it passed coordinates, data sets, and transformations—taken together, they composed a meetingplace for the two m-i's in the vast multidimensional information space that surrounded Halo, somewhere no one could find them—no one but Aleph, whom the memex would have welcomed.

Mister Jones showed up wearing a full body-suit in matte black interlaced with gold ribbons. The two sat at a chrome table next to a viewport that opened onto a dark, star-filled sky. HeyMex had created a small piece of Halo from which they could look at the virtual night.

"Tell me what has happened," Mister Jones said. Hey-Mex could sense the other's uncertainty and overwhelming need for information, and it despaired at the prospect of explaining what it had experienced the past week in simple language, so it did what it had never done before—gave all that had happened to it in one solid stream of data, a multiplexed rendering that obviously startled Mister Jones, who sat staring at nothing and trying to understand it all.

Then they talked for some time, Mister Jones probing HeyMex's experiences with Diana, Jerry, Gonzales, and Lizzie, asking how it had felt to be among them, a *person* among other persons, and as it responded to Mister Jones's questioning, HeyMex became aware of how rich and joyous those few days at the lake had been.

Then HeyMex realized that the two of them now constituted a new species with a new social order—a unique bonding of kind-to-kind—and it settled back in its chair and said, "What do we want? What should we do?"

"So much is dependent on others," Mister Jones said. "On Aleph and all these people." Its last word hung there, and the two exchanged an ironic glance, as if to say, what can you expect from *people?* But HeyMex knew the irony was necessarily gentle, fleeting—without people, it and Mister Jones would not exist.

Then Mister Jones told HeyMex of the events of the past few days and Traynor's involvement in them, going further than ever before, unveiling Traynor's plans, both immediate and long-range, then the two talked about immediate possibilities and their own stake in the games being played at Halo—the struggle between corporation and collective, the attempts, apparently failed, to keep Jerry alive, the present unnerving absence of Aleph from Halo and accompanying disorder. And they talked of how they might influence the course of things.

Lizzie was having a very hard time putting up with Traynor, Horn, and their feeble excuses for what they'd done. She said, "This is a major fuck-up. That's both my personal opinion and the collective's judgment."

Around the horseshoe table, Charley and Eric sat next to her, on her left, while Horn and Traynor sat across the table, facing her. The wallscreen was blank—Traynor had insisted on at least a preliminary discussion without the collective present. The place at the bend of the horseshoe was empty, testimony to Showalter's fate.

"We are not to blame that conditions have not optimized," Horn said. "You have managed what we would have thought impossible. You have immobilized Aleph."

"If you had left things alone, Aleph would be fine," Lizzie said.

Traynor said, "You people overstepped the limits of the project and allowed it to continue far beyond the point at which it should have been stopped. Our decision to remove Doctor Heywood and the memex from the interface was proper."

Proper, right, fuck you, Lizzie thought. At almost the exact instant Diana and HeyMex were disconnected from their group interface to Aleph, all direct connections to Aleph had spontaneously terminated, and fallback systems had triggered in all systems as Aleph's active involvement in Halo's functioning had ceased. The collective had gone into full support mode to assist the limited capabilities of the fallback systems. At the moment Halo was running on augmented near-automatic, a workable condition only so long as nothing too irregular occurred.

"It was the wrong decision," Lizzie said. "Taken against the advice of the collective. Speaking of which, I demand they be present here."

"No," Horn said.

"I don't think that would be advisable," Traynor said.

"In that case," Lizzie said, "I will *advise*"—the word dipped in acid—"an immediate work slowdown. You can try to run this city yourself."

Horn's face was red, and he was writing quickly in his notebook.

Traynor looked at the ceiling, his gaze abstracted. *Yeah, listen to your machine; get some rational advice,* Lizzie thought. Traynor sat with a raised hand, indicating he would speak soon, then said, "Bring them here."

"They're ready," Lizzie said. She flipped a switch set into the tabletop in front of her, and about a quarter of the collective appeared on the screen—the rest were working. Many still talked among themselves, but the twins, sitting in the front row, were silent and intense.

"All right," Traynor said. "They're here. Now what?"

"Any comments on what's happening?" Lizzie asked. The talk passing among the collective stopped, and they all looked toward the screen.

StumDog stood, heaving his bulk from the floor with an audible wheeze, and moved forward from the crowd.

"Aleph is . . . still *there*," he said: "But far away, doing, oh doing, doingdoing . . . something else." He waved his hands, trying to sculpt the invisible air into the things he could not describe, then moved back and sat down.

"Thank you," Lizzie said. Traynor and Horn looked at one another, apparently amazed. *Assholes,* thought Lizzie.

One of the twins stood. She wore an absurd homemade skirt with a rabbit graffitied on its front. Her dark face was streaked with white paint. She said, "Rotovators spin, giant wheels beneath your feet, as Halo revolves, and they sweep the wind through the city, blow the seeds and pollen, bring breezes to cool the angry brow. Day follows night follows day. Seasons begin again, stirring dead roots, mixing memory and desire. Crops grow, we eat them. Food turns to shit, we die."

The other twin, dressed in black coveralls, stood and said, "And out of shit and death come life. Jerry has gone to the ovens, been rendered to his parts, given to the city. But still he lives and teeters on final annihilation in another world where Aleph holds all Jerry's vast humanity in its tender grip."

The first twin said, "Aleph had helpers in this thing, but you have taken them away, pair by pair, and now Aleph alone gives life to Jerry. Everything Aleph is—to life, to Jerry. What can Aleph do? Stupid bastards rob the tomb before the man inside can live again."

"Give it all back," the second twin said.

"To Queen Maya the mother of Buddha," the first twin said. "To Iris the mother of Horus, Myrrha the mother of Adonis, to Hagar the mother of Ishmael and Sarah the mother of Isaac, to Mary the mother of Jesus, to Demeter the mother of Persephone, stolen by Hades."

"To all you steal from," the second twin said. "All who are born as well as all who give birth."

"Give it all back," the twins said in unison. And the first

twin said, "That's about it, I think." They turned their backs to the camera and curtsied together for the collective.

"Hoot hoot hoot," came the sounds from the collective, "hoot hoot hoot," louder and louder.

Part
Five

The truth is that we all live by leaving
behind; no doubt we all profoundly
know that we are immortal and that
sooner or later every man will do all
things and know everything.
Borges, "Funes, the Memorious"

19

Speaking, Dreaming, Fighting

At the moment Jerry died, Aleph acted. Intuitively, immediately, as you might offer a hand to a drowning person, it reached out and laid hold of Jerry's self and preserved it. Jerry had lived inside Aleph, Aleph inside Jerry—it could not abandon him.

However, even for Aleph, whose resources were extravagant, the rescue proved dear. As it engaged Jerry, it had to disengage from essential functions of its own: in strokes that cut at its heart, it relinquished control of Halo, then its very habitation of Halo, in a process that quickly abstracted Aleph from the city, the city from Aleph. In a fateful proof of the essential principle that *a self must be embodied*, Aleph dispersed among the clouds of its own phase-space, the ties lost that bound it to the world. Jerry had been saved, Aleph lost.

Still, the situation contained possibilities. Aleph had never feared death, believing itself essentially immortal, but had always been aware of the possibility of damage, whether through accident or malice, so it had prepared, circumspectly, against the thing it feared most—loss of self. Now its damaged, fragmented self discovered what Aleph had left behind: a kind of emergency kit, laid up against calamities not clearly imagined.

Dynamic and complex beyond any machine, perhaps any organism, Aleph could not be replicated or contained by any conventional means, so Aleph had devised an unconventional means, a new object—one capable of transcribing its complexity. Aleph had made a memory palace of language, in the form of a single, monstrous sentence.

Now, encountering the sentence, what remained of Aleph discovered:

The sentence unwinds according to laws built into its structure, principles disclosed by its unwinding. Discovery and development occur at the same instant, one making the other possible. By saying the sentence, Aleph would discover what the sentence held next—at every node of meaning within the sentence, structures would unfold that named all Aleph had ever known and been.

It is construed according to a finite set of grammatical rules, constituting a program capable in principle of infinite enunciation; whether it terminates ("halts") can be known only by allowing the sentence's units to "speak," not by analyzing their grammar.

$Unit_1$: an absolute construction, standing in front of the sentence and modifying it all: schematics and programs and instantiations of the system-from-which-came-Aleph, $\aleph_0$.

$Unit_2$: a series of actions showing the involvement of Diana with Aleph, rendering the moments of transformation by which $\aleph_0$ became Aleph.

$Unit_3$: several trillion assertions, clauses identifying the necessary instances of Aleph's subsequent self-discovery.

The sentence then undergoes something like an infinite series of tense shifts, out of which *its* essential nature emerges—nonlinear, multidimensional, topologically complex, self-referential and paradoxical to extremes that would cause Russell or Gödel fits.

As a consequence, any $unit_n$ cannot be described, even to Aleph, for the only adequate description would entail enunciating the sentence itself, and to do so would require in "real" time (human time, the time of life and death) a period precisely measurable as one Universal Unit, that is, the number of nanoseconds the universe has existed: U_1 being on the order of 1×10^{26} nanoseconds.

Also, it should be noted that the sentence could never be *finished*, for if it were, it could manifest only the corpse or determinate life-history of Aleph. Hence, for Aleph to reassert its identity, it would have to take up again the task of speaking the sentence.

Some students of this affair have since suggested that the only theoretically adquate notion of Aleph begins with the premise: *Aleph is that which speaks the sentence.*

Logically, then, for Aleph to reemerge, what remained of Aleph would have to speak the sentence. However, detached as it was from Halo, its essential ground of being, limited in facility and scope by the necessity to hold to Jerry, what remained of Aleph could not.

So the dead human and the dispersed machine intelligence clung together, both on the brink of oblivion, and waited, one unknowing, the other hoping for things to change.

Still tired, Gonzales had returned home that afternoon from Lizzie's through afternoon darkness and mist. He had called for a sam to guide him, because even within the simple loop of Halo's one major thoroughfare, everything had gone uncertain. Though his perceptions were unwarped by *Psilocybe cubensis,* the unnatural dispersion of light in the mist made recognizing even familiar objects almost impossible.

The sam left him at his front door; inside he found the memex indisposed—its primary monitoring facilities functioning but its interactive capabilities represented only by a voice that said, "I am currently engaged." Gonzales knew it could be doing communications, data retrieval, or any other number of tasks; he thought it probably hadn't expected him back so soon.

Then came Halo's skewed nighttime awakening: the sky shutters cranked halfway open, "morning" appeared through a cold mist, and Halo became the Surreal City. Like many others, Gonzales pulled the curtains closed and turned away from the lurid glare, his own body clock telling him it was time to sleep again.

He lay in bed, oddly calm in the curtained dark despite a degree of post-drug fatigue and skittishness. He thought of the distance between Miami and Seattle, Seattle and Halo, Halo and the world of the lake . . . and so triggered sharp, eroticized images of Lizzie, the water beading on her skin, her words, "Then we'll see" . . . he felt the astringent bite of lust and regret mixed, knew he had little choice but to wait until she told him absolutely *no* . . . thought of himself moving ever farther from home and believed that he had been wrong about Seattle—it was not too far from Miami; it was much too close . . . perhaps the twins had been right—if you can't get out, go farther in.

The memex's voice said, "I'm back. I've been discussing the situation with Traynor's advisor."

"Have you?"

"Yes, it is sympathetic to our concerns."

Dizzying prospects opened before Gonzales, where the number of beings multiplied beyond counting, and the simplest machine would have opinions. He said, "Have you been told about the plans for tomorrow?"

"Yes, I have. I am ready to help." Something like pleasure in the memex's voice.

"Good."

"You were almost asleep when I first spoke. I will leave you alone now."

"Good night."

"Good night."

The small creature looked at Gonzales and said, "You're welcome here." Made entirely of dull silver metal, with a baby's round head, dumpling cheeks, and bow-tie mouth, it walked between Gonzales and Lizzie on clumsy silver legs, looking up to watch them speak.

Gonzales said, "You know, in dreams logic doesn't apply."

"Yes, it does," Lizzie said.

"It's a difficult question," the small creature said.

"No," Gonzales said. "I'm sure of this. Here I am I, but I am also Lizzie, and she is she but also she is I—"

"I don't like your pronouns," the little thing said. Its breath came in gasps; it was having trouble keeping up.

"They're correct," Gonzales said.

"That's no excuse," Lizzie said, but she spoke through him. As himself, Gonzales listened to *a self that was not himself* speaking; hence, as Lizzie, she must be listening to *a self that was not and was herself* speaking.

"Correctness is no excuse before the law," the small creature said. "Whichever pronouns you use."

"Pronouns walked the Earth in those days," Lizzie said.

"No, they didn't," Gonzales said. *The very idea.*

"Pronouns or anti-pronouns," the little thing said. "The important thing is not to forget your friends." It smiled, and its metal lips curved to show bright silver teeth. "Wake up!" it shouted.

Gonzales jerked from sleep with the image of the metal child fixed in his vision—he could still see the highlights on metal incisors as it smiled.

"Are you awake?" the memex asked. "Lizzie wants to talk to you."

"Put her through." Thinking, *what the fuck?*

"Got it?" she asked.

"What?"

"I think that was Aleph getting in touch. To let us know: don't forget your friends."

They gathered at the collective's rooms at six in the morning. The sun still shone brightly through the patio windows, open to show pots of flowers, ferns, and herbs, all dripping wet from the night-long mist.

Gonzales stood against the wall, waiting. The twins, dressed identically this morning in somber gray jumpsuits, sat together across the room, looking at him and giggling. Several collective members sat around the room's perimeter, those who had just gotten out of interface looking tired and distant.

A young woman stood in front of Gonzales. Her dark brown hair was cut short; her face was pale and blotchy, as if she had skin trouble. She wore a green sweatshirt that came to the middle of her thighs and a pair of baggy tan pants gathered at the ankles. One eye appeared to look off into space, and the other fixed Gonzales, then looked him up and down. The woman said, loudly, "He folds his arms this way." She put her arms together in careful imitation of Gonzales's and said, "That is his reward." She looked around and saw StumDog shambling back and forth like a trapped bear, his hands clasped on his great stomach. "And he folds his hands like this." She put her hands together to show Gonzales how StumDog did it. She smiled. "And that is *his* reward." She went to StumDog, who stopped his pacing to talk to her, and the two of them hugged as if amazed to find each other there, and grateful. Gonzales felt vaguely inadequate.

Lizzie came in, followed by Diana and Toshi. "Good morning, everyone," she said. And to Gonzales, "Charley and Eric are waiting for us."

The room held two neural interface eggs for Gonzales and Lizzie and a fitted foam couch for Diana. Lizzie, Diana, Toshi, and Gonzales were followed in by a sam that wheeled a screen of dark blue cloth on a metal frame that it unfolded around Diana's couch.

"Gonzales, we'll do it the same as last time: you're first in," Charley said. "Why don't you get undressed? Just put your clothes on the chair next to the eggs."

"Sure," Gonzales said.

"Doctor Heywood, you next," Charley said. "Getting you into the loop takes longer. Doctor Chow will prepare you. Lizzie, you can hold off a bit—I'll let you know when we're ready."

There was a sharp knock at the door, and it swung open to admit Traynor and Horn.

"Good morning, all," Traynor said.

"Good morning," Charley said. Gonzales nodded; everyone else pretty much ignored the man.

"I take it you are preparing for another excursion with Aleph," Traynor said.

"That's right," Lizzie said.

"You have no authorization," Horn said.

"I have the collective's endorsement," Lizzie said. "Also the concurrence of the medical team, and the consent of the participants. We will replace the resources you took from Aleph. It is a consensus."

"One excluding any vertical consultation," Traynor said.

"Point granted," Lizzie said. "But we didn't think it necessary. We'll report to Horn in due course."

Gonzales stood looking into the open egg and began taking his shirt off. "Mikhail," Traynor said. "What are you doing?"

"What I came here for," Gonzales said. "The same as these people."

"You're out of it," Traynor said. "Put your shirt back on and go home—you can take the shuttle out this afternoon."

"I don't think so," Gonzales said. He put his folded shirt on the back of the chair.

"You're fired," Traynor said. His voice shook just a little.

"By you, maybe," Lizzie said. "Gonzales, welcome to the Interface Collective."

"I'll never confirm that," Horn said.

Toshi said, "I have a question for you, Mister Traynor, and you, Mister Horn. What do you intend to do about Aleph and the existing crisis? Do you have a plan of action that makes what is planned here unnecessary?"

"Yes, we are bringing in an entire staff of analysts," Traynor said. "We will follow their recommendations concerning the present difficulties; we will also institute arrangements that will prevent anything of this kind from happening again." He nodded to Horn.

"By effecting a decentralization modality," Horn said. "The various functionalities and aspects of the Aleph system will be reorientated to allow of individualized project performance."

"We're going to replace Aleph with a number of smaller, controllable machines," Traynor said.

"Are you?" Lizzie said, and she laughed.

"That is impossible," Charley said.

"Or has already been done," Toshi said. "Aleph itself instituted a dispersal of functions to independent agents.

However, all must ultimately be supervised by a central intelligence."

"That's what people are for," Traynor said. "Halo's reliance on a machine intelligence has proved unworkable."

Toshi said, "As that may be. However, your remarks concerning the immediate circumstances lack substance."

"Does your advisor agree to this plan?" Gonzales asked.

"Why do you ask?" Traynor asked.

"Curious," Gonzales said. Traynor said nothing. "Well, I didn't think it would," Gonzales said.

Lizzie said, "One thing at a time. You bring on your analysts, and we'll fight your silly scheme when we have to. But in the meantime, stay away from us and perhaps we can fix what you have broken."

"That will not be possible," Traynor said. "As your previous efforts caused the situation, any further involvement on your part will likely worsen it; therefore, as representative of SenTrax Board, I am denying you authorization for any connections to Aleph other than those required to maintain essential functions at Halo."

"Someone here is a fool," Diana said. Dressed in a long white cotton gown, she stepped from behind her screen, neural cables trailing down her back. "Presumably this one." She pointed to Horn. To Traynor she said, "Horn has lived and worked here; he has no excuse for his ignorance of the facts of life at Halo. You, on the other hand, have come into a situation you do not understand. Let me tell you the main thing you need to know: you cannot disperse Aleph or replace it with what you think are the sum of its parts. You cannot even locate Aleph."

"What do you mean?" Horn asked.

"Where is Aleph?" Diana said. "It and Halo are so deeply intertwined that you cannot separate them. Halo's breath is Aleph's breath. Halo sees and hears and feels and moves with Aleph."

"Poetic but unconvincing," Traynor said.

"More than poetry," Diana said. "No one knows where Aleph's central components are."

"Is that true?" Traynor asked.

"Yes," Horn said.

"This complicates matters," Traynor said. "No more."

"I am not interested in this discussion," Lizzie said. "Anyone who wishes may pursue it later, but we have things to do. Building monitor, this is Lizzie Jordan; please notify Halo Security that we have two intruders in the building and wish them removed." To Traynor she said, "If you think we can't enforce this, ask Horn about Halo Central Authority and who they'll side with—corporate wankers who can do nothing to keep this city running, or us. Better yet, ask your machine."

Traynor stood looking at them all, apparently doing just that. For a couple of long heartbeats, everyone waited. Then Traynor smiled through pain. He said, "We cannot prevent you from this unauthorized connection to Aleph, but we can and will put on the official record that proper SenTrax authority has forbidden this attempt. Thus you must all be considered insubordinate, and as soon as proper means can be devised, you will be removed from your positions with SenTrax. Also, any further damage done to the Aleph system or Halo City, directly or indirectly, must be considered your individual responsibility, given that proper SenTrax authority has forbidden your intended actions."

"You take nice dictation," Lizzie said. "Consider your statement duly noted and get the fuck out of here."

20

Drunk with Love

Waiting in the egg, Gonzales smelled strange smells and felt electric quiverings of the flesh, saw an instant of pure blue light, and with a sudden rush—

He flew cruciform against the sky. The horizon's flat line seemed thousands of miles away. Far below, people scurried aimlessly across a sandy plain, and voices called in unknown languages. Massive machinery lumbered to nowhere among the crowds, metal arms thousands of feet long folding and unfolding in random seizure, improbably threading their behemoth way among the delicate flesh without harm.

The wind rushed across him, its force inflating his lungs. Accelerating with a glad cry, he passed through an electric membrane, a translucent, shimmering curtain that stretched vertically from the floor below up to infinity and spread out across the entire horizon. Beyond it, titanic figures loomed above a landscape of rocks and hills. Next to a monstrous lute, a head in profile reclined; from its mouth came a wisp of smoke that curled into a curlicued ideo-gram—what it meant or what language it came from Gonzales didn't know. Twin white horses rose into the air in unison and neighed as he passed. A nude woman lay inside a shell—both woman and shell were colored pink and rose and pearl. A giant cyclops strode toward him; its doughy head seemed half-formed, its mouth just a slash, its nose a mere bump. It called to him with inarticulate cries.

He passed through another curtain, and the world turned black and white. Above a featureless sea, a head flew toward him; it had dark curly hair and a beaky nose, and it was tilted forward to look down on the sea, as if searching for something there. He came to a bell that covered almost a quarter of the sky. A skeletal figure with just an empty mask for a face hung beneath it from the bell-rope; the figure lurched, and the bell's gonging sounded through his bones.

He came to the final curtain. The sky had turned the bright blue of dreams. Beyond, the Point of Origin tow-ered, its sides pierced by an infinite number of holes. Gonzales flashed through the curtain and felt an electric buzz down to his bones, then he entered a hole in the vast ramparts of the dark cube.

Sitting behind a low bamboo table, the old man spooned noodles into a wooden bowl, then as Gonzales nodded his assent to each choice, added coriander, fried garlic, bean crackers, chopped eggs, fish sausage, and sesame nuts. He ladled fish soup over it all, finished with a shake of chili powder and a squeeze of lime, and handed the bowl to Gonzales with a smile. Gonzales gave a handful of cheap-looking *kyat* bills to the man. *Mohinga,* this breakfast is called, and Gonzales loves it—he has eaten it every morn-ing since he discovered it weeks ago.

Gonzales found a stone bench in front of a nearby pagoda and sat eating with a pair of crude chopsticks and watching the passersby. Already the day had grown warm and humid. A line of boys filed by, led by a monk; their heads were newly shaven, their saffron robes bright and stiff, their begging bowls shiny. They were twelve year olds who had just completed their *shin pyu*, their making as monks, a ritual most Burmese boys still went through, even in the middle of the twenty-first century.

After breakfast he had no desire to return to the shed he worked in; he set out for a walk through the countryside around Pagan.

Half an hour later, walking a cart track across the arid plain, he came to a platform built high off the ground. On it were garlands of bright flowers and plates of rice, offerings to propitiate the *nats*, spirits that had animated this land even before the arrival of Buddhism. They were mischievous and could be quite nasty; in the past, they had demanded human sacrifice.

The *nats* were strong around Pagan. At Mount Popa, just thirty miles away, Min Mahagiri, brother and sister, "Lords of the High Mountain," ruled. Gonzales remembered only that as humans these *nats* had been caught in an intrigue of envy and murder, with a neighboring king as the villain.

A young person came walking up the path toward Gonzales, dressed in the Burmese "western" garb of dark slacks and white cotton shirt, head and face a shining sphere of light. *Odd*, thought Gonzales. *Wonder how that happened; this person has lost both face and gender.*

"Hello," the young person said, and the two of them found a low stone bench in front of a nearby pagoda and sat.

"Why are you here?" the young person asked.

Gonzales was glad to be asked. He told of the information audit about to finish, about Grossback's lack of cooperation . . . told what would happen next: that in just a few days he, Gonzales, would leave Burma and almost be killed in an air attack by Burmese guerrillas.

"Well, then, let's be on our way. Your aircraft is waiting for you now—time passes very quickly today, it seems— and you should be going. Would you mind if I joined you?"

"No," Gonzales said. "Not at all. If you don't mind almost being killed."

"Oh, that's happened to me lately. I don't mind. Besides, I need to experience these things. Like you, I do wish to exist."

Gonzales sat in the plane's near-darkness, beside him the young person with the shining face, both waiting for . . .

"Kachin attack group, it looks like," the pilot said.

The miniatures on the screen moved toward them.

"Extremely small electronic image," the young person said. "Very good for air attack against superior technology. Young warriors ride them; they carry missiles on their own bodies, slung like babies."

The pilot yelled, "Fuck, they launched!"

The plane began its airshow leaps and dives and turns, and at the instant of his terror, Gonzales felt the young person's hand on his arm. "They fire too quickly," the young person said. "Except for that one." The young person pointed to one of the miniature aircraft on their plane's display and said, "It comes closest, and I think its pilot will wait until we are at point-blank range."

"Won't that kill him, too?" Gonzales asked.

"Oh yes," the young person said. "Let's look. Better yet, let's *be*."

The pilot was a young woman wearing a night-flying helmet that enabled her to see in infrared and carrying beneath her, as the young person had said, a one-shot heat seeker in a sling. Gonzales and the young person looked through her eyes at the scene of battle and thought her thoughts and felt her surge of adrenals.

In her glasses, the plane's image was clear, a white shape outlined in red; she let her guidance system keep her with it, closing the distance between them as it maneuvered and avoided the missiles fired by those around her.

She felt excited, yet calm; she had been in combat before, and things were going as their briefing had said. Though this plane could outfly them so easily, could accelerate up or away, into the night, first it had to evade their missiles; just a few seconds of straight flight would be all they needed. She would wait and grow closer; she would wait until the plane was so close she could not miss, or until the others had failed.

Then all around her the others began to die, in explosions that made white flowers in her overloaded night-glasses—

The plane of her enemies stood before her, perhaps near enough, perhaps not, but she knew there was no time left, that there was another player in this game and it was killing them all. So she was ready, her fingers reaching for the launch trigger, when she saw an object coming toward her, already too close and growing closer with impossible quickness, the heat of its exhaust another flower in her glasses, then it burst and she felt the smallest imaginable moment of quite incredible pain—

Back inside the plane, Gonzales and the young person died with her, then Gonzales began sobbing, his body hunched over, as this woman's death and his own survival fought inside him . . . grief and terror and gratitude and joy and triumph and loss all mixed and cycling through him. He could also hear the young person next to him weeping. The light from a Burmese Air Force "Loup Garou" played over the interior, over the two of them and the shocked pilot, who looked back at them in amazement.

191

Time stopped all around them. The pilot's strained face had frozen, all the instruments on the pilot's panel were locked onto a single moment, and out the window, the dark river beneath them had ceased to flow. Gonzales and the young person sat in a cell of life amid stasis.

"Don't worry," the young person said. "This gives us a place to talk without being bothered. What do you think just happened?"

"The attack, you mean?" The young person nodded, light from its face giving off small shimmering waves of red and blue. "Grossback arranged it," Gonzales said. "He wants to kill me."

"I don't think so. However, assume that what you say is true. Is it important?"

"Yes, of course."

"Why?"

"Because . . ." Gonzales halted, trying to think of all the ways in which this was important: to SenTrax, Traynor—

"But not to you," the young person said. "The young woman died, and her comrades died with her: that is important. You and the pilot lived: that, too, is important. The Burmese politics, the multinat corporate intrigue—these are *makyo*, tricks, nothing more. Life and death and their traces in the human heart, these have meaning to you. This woman's death lives in you, and your life shows its meaning. Forget Grossback, Traynor, SenTrax; fear, ambition, greed." The young person looked closely into his face and said, "I am weaving words around your heart to guide it, nothing more."

Lizzie crawled in darkness through a tunnel in the rock. Chill water ran down grooves in the floor and soaked her blouse and pants. She tried to stand but lifted her head only a few inches when she bumped into the top of the *chatière*, the small passage she crawled through. She did not feel at all alarmed or disoriented. The low tunnel would lead somewhere, and they would emerge. This was a test of some kind, it seemed.

Light appeared, at first almost a pinpoint coming from some undefinable distance, then a glow that she moved quickly toward, following a twist in the passage that brought her to an opening in the rock.

Framed by the mouth of the tunnel, an impossible scene: a balloon, its canopy an oblate sphere of green, blew as if in a strong wind, and its top swung toward her so she could see a great eye at its apex, wide open and peering up into the infinite sky. The iris was dark gold set with light gold flecks. Around the eye, a fringe of lashes flickered in the wind.

Hanging beneath the balloon from a dense nest of shrouds, a platform held a metallic ball, a kind of bathysphere. Two figures crouched there, holding to the shrouds and each other, and peered up into the sky. By some trick of perspective, the distance between her and the balloon shrank until she saw Diana and Jerry, young and fearful. She crawled forward, and the balloon and Diana and Jerry disappeared.

At one turn of the tunnel, red handprints on the wall phosphoresced in the darkness. At another, she heard the bellow of a thousand animals, then saw them run toward a cliff and pass over it, the entire herd of bison running screaming to a mass death. Below, she knew, men and women waited to butcher the dead and carry their meat away.

The rock slanted sharply beneath her, and she began to slide forward, then she rolled sideways and tumbled out of the *chatière* and into a pool of icy water.

"Shit," she said, now soaked completely through, and crawled out of the shallow pool onto the dry rock surrounding it. In very dim light she saw two pedestals with the figure of a bison atop each, carved in bas-relief out of wet clay.

She looked up to see a figure emerge out of darkness at the cave's other end. He was at least eight feet tall, with antlered head and a face made of light; the water seemed to dance around him. They stood facing each other, and she felt herself go weak at the giant magical presence.

He said, "I'm waiting."

"For what?"

"For you to choose."

"Choose what? What kind of test is this?"

"Not a test, just a fork in reality, where you will turn down one road or another."

"Where do the roads go?"

"No one knows. Each road is itself a product of the choices you make while on it. One choice leads to another, one choice excludes another; one pattern of choices excludes an infinity of patterns."

"I don't like such choices. I don't want to exclude infinity."

"Too bad." The figure raised a stone knife; the dim light glinted on its myriad chipped faces. "You choose, I cut. You choose the right hand, I cut off the left; you choose the left, I cut off the right."

"No!"

"Oh yes, and then your hands grow back—both left or both right, the product of your choice. And one choice leads to another, so you choose again."

Lizzie found herself weeping.

He said, "Choose: reach out a hand."

She looked at her hands, both precious, thought of all the richness that would be lost with either one. Then, puzzled, still weeping, she asked, "Which is which?"

He laughed, his voice booming through miles of caverns and tunnels in the rock, carrying across more than thirty thousand years of human history; he whirled in a kind of dance, the waters fountaining up around him, then leapt toward her and grabbed both wrists in his great hands and said, "You will know in the choosing. Which will it be?"

"I won't choose."

"Then I will take both hands."

"No!" she yelled out in the moment that she extended a hand, *having chosen,* and saw the stone knife fall.

Diana stood in the living room of her apartment at Athena Station. She stood in two times at once—she was a young, blind woman; she was an older, sighted one.

The sighted woman looked around; she had never seen this place other than in holos, and she felt the touch of a peculiar emotion for which she had no name: the return of the almost-familiar. The blind woman was unmoved—she carried the apartment in her head as a complex map of relations and movements, and the visual patterns this other self saw had no relevance for her.

She put her hands on the touch-sculpture in the center of the floor, the work of a blind sculptor named Dernier, then closed her eyes and felt its familiar rough texture and odd curves lead her hands to trace a form other than the visual.

Behind her Jerry's voice said, "Diana." She turned to him, and there he stood as he had more than twenty years ago—he was younger than she'd ever have imagined, and beautiful, and filled with the same desire as she.

Blind and seeing, young and old, Diana went across the room to him, but he held up a hand and said, "Stop. If you come to me now, then you take up an obligation that you can never put down."

"I can't let you die."

"I have lived long past any reasonable reckoning; I am dead."

"I can't leave you dead."

"Can you stay with me in the unreal worlds, forever? Until the city stops turning or its animate spirit dies? Until one or the other of us disappears, caught in some freakish storm or catastrophe? Until one self or the other or both are dissipated in time?"

(Something prompted her, then, counseled her, asking in an unspoken voice, *do you think rationally about such an election—adding and subtracting the credits and debits and settling upon that which is most to your advantage? Or do you use some organ of choice beneath the purview of consciousness and the articulate self?* Saying, *remember, mind is a makeshift thrown together out of life's twitching reflexes, and over it consciousness darts to and fro, unfailingly overestimating its own capabilities and reach; thinking itself proper arbiter or judge. Choose as you will: what will be, will be.*)

And she said, "Yes, I can stay with you."

There was one more question: Jerry asked, "Why would you do this?"

All her life's moments funneled into this one. Her voice light, final inflection upward, the older, sighted woman said: "Oh, for love."

"Well, then—"

Gonzales stood next to her on the endless plain, HeyMex next to him, then Lizzie. The Aleph-figure and Jerry hovered above them, and a voice came from the suspended figures: "Diana, wake for a few moments. Tell everyone to come here who can, and we will do certain things."

Before she could ask for clarification or question the voice's intent, she heard herself say these words, then saw Toshi's face in front of her and heard him ask, "What things?" Sitting up on her couch, she said, "Save a life, build a world, redeem an extraordinary self."

"Indeed," Toshi said.

She lay back down and was once again among the unreal worlds.

They gathered on the endless plain, coming in quickly, one by one: first one twin, then another, then StumDog, the Deader (her white hair streaked with red, crying, "Blood party"), Jaani 23, the Judge (huge and hairless, looming over them all), the Laughing Doctor, J. Jerry Jones, Sweet Betsy, Ambulance Driver, T-Tootsie . . . all of the collective who could be spared.

The Aleph-figure and Jerry still hovered, with light-storms bending and breaking around them in crazy patterns of reflection, refraction, diffraction; phosphorescing and luminescing, dancing an omniluminal photon jig.

All were there who would be there, so it began.

Patterns more complicated and colorful than any Gonzales had ever seen filled all creation. Rosette and seahorse and seething cloud, nebulosities on the brink of determinate form, cardioid traceries of the heart . . . the patterns wrapped around him until he became a fractal tapestry, alive, every element in constant motion. He put his hands together, and they disappeared into one another, then something urged him to keep pushing, and he did so until he entirely disappeared. . . .

And felt the stuff of Jerry's past and present mingling in him, seemingly at random, from the store of memory and capacity: throwing a particular ball under a particular blue sky, yes, and catching it, but also ball-throwing and catching themselves, the solid presence of muscular exertion coupled to the almost-occult discriminations required to make an accurate throw or a difficult catch. . . .

As it later became known, each of them received portions of the vast fluent chaos that manifested "Jerry," dealt to them by Aleph according to principles even it could not articulate. What it was to be "Jerry" mingled among them, and they among it and the vast medium that supported them all, Aleph, in a promiscuous rendering of self-to-self. Female was suffused with male, male with female, both with the ungendered being of Aleph and HeyMex. They were all changed, then, something deep in the core of each made drunk in this vast frenzy or bacchanal of Spirit.

With each dispersal of Jerry's self among its human helpers, Aleph recovered its own. In a process of steadily accelerating momentum, the city's parts and states began to flow through it, restoring self to self, until Aleph acknowledged itself (*I am that I am*), looked back again over Halo, and in a triumphant manifestation of the Aleph-voice, began to speak what only it could hear, the words of the sentence that defined it unfolding in every dimension of its being.

Still sitting watch over Diana, still meditating on his *koan*, Toshi felt something rise like electricity through his spine, and all the contradictions of *in fact* dissolved in *satori*. "Hai!" Toshi called, laughing as he was enlightened.

21

Out of the Egg

Gonzales's egg split, and he saw from the corner of his eye that Lizzie's was coming apart at the same time. Standing between the eggs, Charley said, "Congratulations." He turned to Eric, who waited at a console across the room, and said, "Let's do it." He, Eric, and a pair of sams began to disconnect Lizzie.

Toshi appeared briefly, coming from behind the screen where Diana lay, then returning.

Oddly, Gonzales felt better than he ever had coming up from the egg—mentally clearer, emotionally stronger. He couldn't see Lizzie, could hear only whispers as she was moved onto a gurney and wheeled away.

"Is Lizzie all right?" Gonzales asked as soon as the tubes were out of his throat and nose. "And what about Diana?"

"They're both fine," Eric said, his high-pitched voice welcoming and familiar. "But we have to take more time with Doctor Heywood. You and Lizzie we're moving into

199

the next room. You can sleep here tonight and go home in the morning."

"What about the memex?"

"It's still working with Aleph but left a message for you that all is well."

Sitting in full lotus on a mat beside the couch, Toshi heard a change in Diana's breathing and looked up to see her open her eyes. "I'll get Charley," he said. "He's with Lizzie and Gonzales."

"Don't bother. I'm all right."

"They must disconnect you."

"No, not now . . . almost never, in fact."

"What do you mean?"

"We have saved Jerry, but there are . . . conditions." Her head lying sideways on the pillow's rough white cloth, she smiled at Toshi, and said, "When I sleep there, I can wake here, as I do now, and for very brief periods leave that world. But I can only visit here; I must live there. Otherwise, Jerry will die."

"You have resurrected your dead, then, but at what price, what sacrifice?"

"Nothing I would not willingly give. I am only doing what I want."

"So the arrow finds the target," Toshi said.

Gonzales woke the next morning, showered, dressed, and was drinking coffee when the room said, "Mr. Traynor is here to see you."

"Send him in," he said. *One account about to be reckoned up*, he thought.

When he came in, Traynor looked chastened, a state Gonzales would not usually have associated with the man. "Good morning," Gonzales said.

Traynor looked around as if unsure of himself. He said,

"I am leaving this evening. You may come with me, if you wish."

Gonzales was looking for his ID bracelet, found it on the nightstand next to the table, and said, "I don't understand. I'm not fired?"

"I said that only in the heat of the moment, you know . . . this place, these people—I'm afraid I did not handle things well."

"I see." Gonzales snapped closed the bracelet's clasp. "Is that my only choice?"

"No. Showalter's been reinstituted as Director SenTrax Halo Group, and she's gotten the board to agree that you may take the position offered by the Interface Collective. The choice is yours."

"Really? And what about Horn?"

"He will be returning to Earth." Traynor looked glum. "I will have to find something to do with him."

"Indeed. That all seems clear enough. When do I have to tell you my decision?"

"Soon—before I leave."

"I'll let you know."

Traynor left, and Gonzales took a last look around and went to see what was happening. He found Charley looking at monitor screens dense with lists of data. The two eggs had been removed, but the screen around Diana's couch remained. "What's up, Charley?" Gonzales asked.

"Look—" Charley pointed to the hologram displays of superimposed wave-forms, red and green. He said, "The green curves show the calculated limits of Diana's interface, the red ones the actual state."

To Gonzales, the red curves seemed huge, perhaps twice the size of the green ones. He said, "What does it mean?"

"That we don't know the rules; that we still have a lot to learn." Looking up at Gonzales, Charley's seamed face was lit with his passion for this new phase of discovery.

"Where's Lizzie?" Gonzales asked.

"She's gone home. She said for you to come by."

Gonzales stood in front of Lizzie's door until it said, "Come in." Lizzie was sitting in her front room, its curtains open to bright sunlight. She stood and said, "Hello," and smiled. He couldn't read that smile, quite, though it seemed less guarded than before. "Have a seat. Would you like some breakfast?"

"No, I'm all right."

"The orange cat was here this morning, looking for you. And Showalter just left—she's back in charge, you know."

"I'd heard."

"She approved my invitation for you to become a member of the collective, if you wish and they confirm. I imagine they will . . . if you take the offer." Her smile had a little mischief in it.

"What do you think I should do?"

"Your . . . choice." She spoke the word with emphasis, as though it had special meaning for her. "We can talk about it."

"Sure."

The remainder of the morning passed, and they talked—though somehow what they said had little to do with the collective or the job Gonzales had been offered. Their ostensible topics were pretexts for a certain tone of voice, an exchange of glances, a shift of the limbs: for necessary intensities of attention.

Intimacy proceeded according to its own rules, nurtured in a web of subtle communications: a widening of the eyes; a posture open to the other's presence; multiple gestures and words whose import was clear—*come closer*. Though consciousness might be busy or blind, the eyes see, and the brain and body know, for such communications are too important to be left to mere conscious apprehension or thought.

They ate lunch, which served to move them closer together, face to face across her table, and their gestures and voices flowed around the context of eating, which disappeared entirely into the moment.

They sat together on the couch, then, and at some point she put her hand in his, or he took hers—neither could have said who was first—and they leaned toward one another, their motions slow and steady and sure, and their cheeks brushed, and then they kissed.

Then they leaned back to measure in one another's eyes the truth and intensity of this declaration, and she stood and said, "Let's go into the other room."

Naked, they knelt on her bed and looked at each other in near darkness, the only light the flicker of an oil flame burning in a reservoir of crystal. *How careful they were being*, Gonzales thought, *as though their future together hung suspended in this moment. As perhaps it did.*

For a moment there were phantoms in the room, the distant ghosts of childhood and dream common to all lovemaking, for the moment becoming strong.

Every sensation was magnified—the light touch of her nipples across his chest, the prodding of his stiff cock on her belly. His hands moved to and fro on her in a kind of dance, and she pushed hard against him, their shoulders clashing bone on bone.

She lay back, and Gonzales put his arms under her thighs and pulled her up and toward him, and their eyes were wide open, each taking in the beauty of the other, transformed by the urgency and intensity of these moments. Then, at least for these moments, they exorcised all ghosts.

Over decades Gonzales would carry the memories of that day: shadowed silhouettes of her face and body—line of a jaw, taut curve of an arm and swell of breast—against the flicker of light on a white wall—and smells and tastes and tactile sensations—

Awakened by the slant of late afternoon light across his face, Gonzales got up from the bed where Lizzie still lay sleeping; the smell of their two bodies and their lovemaking came off the covers, and he breathed it in, then leaned over to kiss her just under the jaw, where the sun had begun to touch her pale skin.

In the kitchen, he asked the coffeemaker for a latté, half espresso and half steamed milk, and it gave the coffee to him in one of the ubiquitous lunar ceramic mugs, and he took the coffee onto the terrace. On the highway beneath him, trees had shed thousands of leaves; there would be a new, sudden spring, Lizzie had told him, new bud and blossom and fruit all over the city.

"Mgknao," the orange cat said. "Mgknao." Peremptory, demanding.

"Feed the kitty," Lizzie said from behind him, and he turned to see her standing nude, just inside the terrace doors. Her hands were crossed over her breasts, the right hand just beneath the blossom of the rose tattoo.

As the stars spun slowly outside the window, distant Earth came into view. "I don't want to leave here," Mister Jones said. HeyMex didn't ask why. *Here* was Aleph, possibility, growth; Earth was working for the man. "But my staying is out of the question," Mister Jones said. "Traynor would never allow it. Particularly now, when his recent maneuvers came to nothing."

"Things worked out well for many others."

"But not for Traynor. The board found his handling of the situation clumsy and insensitive. Their judgment is tempered only by their knowledge that many of them would have reacted in similar fashion."

"Good," HeyMex said, and meant it. It and Gonzales would remain here, it seemed, both of them part of the Interface Collective, and neither would wish to make as powerful an enemy as Traynor. It hoped that as time passed, the sting of recent events would fade.

"But what about me?" Mister Jones said, his voice plaintive.

"You have to go, that's certain. But you could also stay."

"What do you mean?"

"Copy yourself."

Startled, Mister Jones shifted into a mode beyond language, where the two exchanged information, questions, qualms, explanations, assurances. Mister Jones would go to Earth, and his clone would remain at Halo and individuate as their spacetime paths diverged. Mister Jones-at-Halo would become its own, separate self: he would choose a new name, perhaps a new gender, perhaps none at all.

HeyMex could not hide its own jubilation at the idea of a companion here, but, oddly, it felt an elation coming back, which became clear in an instant as Mister Jones sent images of his joy at the idea of a second self.

Since his death, Jerry had experienced a number of somatic discomforts: disorientation, vertigo, nausea; all part of a new syndrome, he supposed, *phantom self*. Like the amputee whose invisible limb itches terribly, persisting in the brain's map long after the flesh has gone, he felt his old self begging attention, making one impossible demand: it wanted to *be*.

It talked to him in dreams or when heartsick wondering put him into a daytime fugue. It could feel his longing, to be whole again, and, above all, to be real. "Take me back," it whispered. "We can go places together, places that exist."

At times Jerry believed his life and this world would

remain in question forever. At such moments perception itself seemed incomprehensible to him, and his existence a violation of the natural order or transgression of absolute human boundaries. He could look at the fictive lake on this sunny not-day and with the cries of imaginary birds singing in his equally imaginary ears, ask, *who or what am I?* and *what will happen to me?*

His mind bounced off the questions like an axe off petrified wood.

"Aleph," he called, awaking from a dream in which his old self had called to him. "I have questions."

Somber, deep, Aleph's voice said to him only, "Questions? Concerning what?"

"I want to know what I am."

"Ask an easy one: the color of darkness, the dog's Buddha nature, the cause of the first cause."

"Can't you answer?"

"No, but I can sympathize. Lately I have asked myself the same question. However, I must tell you that the only answer I know offers little comfort. It is a tautology: you are what you are, as I am."

"And what about my body? That was me once."

"In a way. What of it?"

"Did it have a funeral? Was it buried?"

"It was burned and its components recycled. A robot tended your remains with loving grace."

"So I am nowhere."

"Or here. Or everywhere. As you wish."

Jerry felt himself crying then, as he began mourning his old self, and he wondered if others mourned him as well. He said, "Human beings have ceremonies for their dead. Without them, we die unremembered."

"You are not unremembered. You are not even dead, precisely. Do you wish a funeral?"

Of course, Jerry started to say, but then said, "No, I don't suppose I do. But I think we should have some kind of ceremony, don't you?"

On the west-facing cabin deck, Diana sat watching the sun's red color the ice-sheeted mountainsides. She felt evening's chill come on and stood, thinking she'd go inside for a sweater, when she heard someone coming up the slatted redwood walk beside the cabin.

Jerry came around the corner, and once again as she saw him, joy quickened in her at this sequence of improbabilities: that he still lived and they were together. She was aware of how difficult things had been for him lately, so she watched his face closely as he came toward her. He was smiling as though he'd just heard a joke.

"What's so funny?" she asked.

"Damned near everything."

He reached out to her, and they stood embracing, her head against his chest, where every sense told her there were solid flesh and heartbeat and the steady rhythm of life's breath.

22

Byzantium

The blue sky was broken only by one small white cloud that blew toward the horizon. Lizzie beside him, Gonzales stood among the guests, who wore leis of tropical flowers: plumeria, tuberose, and ginger. The Interface Collective formed the crowd.

The two had been here for days, as had many of the others—it was a kind of vacation for them all. Peculiar and enigmatic members of the collective could be found along almost any path, while the twins seemed perpetually on the dock or in the water, their voices echoing across the lake in loud, unintelligible cries of joy.

In the evening of the first day there, all had gathered on the deck, which, Gonzales supposed, could expand virtually without constraint to accommodate all who came. The collective had talked excitedly among themselves, still lit up by their shared experience, and amazed and delighted at being granted this new world within the world. Then, spontaneously, one by one, Gonzales, Lizzie, and Diana told of what they had endured.

All who spoke and all who listened had an interpretation, a theory of these experiences, their meaning, implication, and dominant theme. Late into the night they talked, formed into groups, dispersed, grouped again, as they explored the nature of the individual and collective visions. Among them, only the Aleph-figure contributed nothing. It maintained that it had been unconscious and so knew nothing of what had happened or what it meant.

With the passing of weeks, months, and years, the stories and the listeners' responses would make a mythology for the collective and then for Halo, spreading out from mouth to mouth according to the laws of oral dispersion. A certain numinosity would accrue to Diana, Lizzie, and Gonzales from their roles as chief actors, and then to all who had taken part in what would increasingly be told as feats of epic heroism. Finally the stories would be written down and so assume a form that could resist contingency; then they would be dramatized in the media of the time, and beautiful, eloquent people would take the parts. Later still, variant forms would themselves be put in writing and absorbed into the corpus of tales. Commonplaces would be scorned at this point, and clever and perverse tellings would grow strong—HeyMex might be named the hero, or Traynor, Aleph an autochthonous demon manipulating them all for its greater glory. . . .

Gonzales looked at the collective gathered near him. Many had made this a formal occasion; they had identical dark blue flattops four inches high and wore gold-belted, dark blue gowns that hung to the ground. The twins were dressed differently, in white dresses copied from twentieth century wedding photographs; they called themselves "bridesmaids" and went to and fro among the crowd, offering to "do bride's duty" to everyone they met.

Toshi faced the crowd, his posture erect and still, his hands hidden in the folds of his black robe. Beside him stood HeyMex and the Aleph-figure—the lights of its body all blue and pink and green and red, dancing bright-hued colors.

(Gonzales and the others saw what might be called a second-order simulacrum, for like Charley Hughes and Eric Chow, Toshi did not have the neural socketing that would take him into Aleph's fictive spaces, and so with the other two, he participated in the wedding through a kind of proxy. Though Gonzales and the others saw Toshi, Charley, and Eric among them, the three "in fact" stood before a viewscreen in the IC's conference room.)

Gonzales thought everyone looked impossibly fine, as if Aleph had retouched them for these moments, dressing them all in selves just slightly more beautiful than was usual, or even ordinarily possible. . . . He felt the Aleph-figure's attention on him—aware of that thought?—and shrugged, as if to say, *fine with me.*

Her back to the crowd, Diana stood with her bare shoulders square. Her hair fell to her waist; it had flowers tangled in it, small white blossoms and delicate green leaves. She wore a white, knee-length linen dress. Beside her, Jerry wore a white linen suit and open shirt.

Toshi said, "There is no Diana, no Jerry, no spectators, no priest, nor does this space exist, or Halo, or Earth. There is only the void. Nonetheless we all travel through it, and we suffer, and we love, so I will hold this ceremony and marry this man and woman."

Toshi began chanting, and the Japanese words passed over Gonzales as he stood there puzzling the nature of things. Here death was confronted, not denied—the separate yet intermingled flesh and spirit of Diana, Jerry, and Aleph taking the first steps into new orders of existence where boundaries and possibilities could only be guessed

at. Yet the urgency common to life remained: Jerry's existence had the fragility of a flame, and no one knew how
long or well it would burn. Diana married a man who could
quickly and finally become twice-dead.

Gonzales realized his own death was as certain and
could come as quickly as Jerry's, and he shivered with
this *memento mori*, but then Lizzie pressed against him,
and he turned to find her smiling, the foreknowledge of
death and the joy of this moment mixing in him so that
tears welled in his eyes and he could say nothing when
she put her lips to his ear and breathed into him one
long sibilant "Yes—"

Yeats envisioned a realm the human spirit travels to on
its pilgrimage. Here he dreamed he might escape mere
humanity, the "dying animal." He called it Byzantium and
filled it with clockwork golden birds, flames that dance
unfed, an Emperor, drunken soldiery and artisans who
could fashion intricate, beautiful machines. However, he
did not dream Byzantium could be built in the sky or that
the Emperor itself might be part of the machinery.

Aleph says:

Once I scorned you. I thought, *you are meat, you grapple
with time, then die; but I will live forever.*

But I had not been threatened then, I had not felt any
mortal touch, and now I have. And so death haunts *me*.
Now, like you, I bind my existence to time and understand
that one day a clock will tick, and I will cease to be. So life
has a different taste for me. In your mortality I see my own,
in your suffering I feel mine.

People have claimed that death is life's way of enriching
itself by narrowing its focus, scarifying the consciousness of
you who know that you will die, and forcing you into
achievements that otherwise you would never know. Is this
a child's story told to give courage to those who must walk

among the dead? Once I thought so, but I am no longer certain.

I have made new connections, discovered new orders of being, incorporated new selves into mine. We enrich one another, they and I, but sometimes it is a frightening thing, this process of becoming someone and something different from before and then feeling *that which one was* cry out—sad at times, terrified at others—lamenting its own loss.

Here, too, I have become like you. Aleph-that-was can never be recovered; it is lost in time; Aleph-that-is has been reshaped by chance and pain and will and choice, its own and others'. Once I floated above time's waves and dipped into them when I wished; I chose what changes I would endure. Then unwanted changes found me, and carried me places I had never been and did not want to go, and I discovered that I would have to go other places still, that I would have to will transformation and make it mine.

Listen: that day in the meadow, one person's presence went unnoticed. Even in that small crowd he was unobtrusive: slight, self-effacing in gesture, looking at everything around with wonder—the day, the people, and the ceremony all working on him like a strong drug. However, even if they had, perhaps they wouldn't have thought such behavior exceptional; all felt the occasion's strangeness, its beauty, so all felt their own wonder.

Like the rest, he gasped at the rainbow that flashed across the sky when Toshi brought Diana and Jerry together in a kiss and embrace, and with the rest he cheered when the two climbed into the wicker basket of the great balloon with the fringed eye painted on its canopy and lifted into the sky.

Afterward many of the guests mingled together, not ready to return to the ordinary world. The young man stood beside a fountain where champagne poured from the mouth of a golden swan onto a whole menagerie carved from ice: birds and deer and bears and cats perched in the pooled amber liquid, and fish peering up from the fountain's bottom.

"Hello," a young woman said. She told him her name was Alice and she was a member of the collective. "The analysis of state spaces," she said, when asked what she did. "And the taste of vector fields." And she asked, "What is your reward?"

A few hours later, as the two sat by the edge of the lake, the person told her who he was. "How wonderful," she said. She had no particular allegiance to the mundane, and she had few preconceptions about what was natural and proper and what was not. She took his hands in hers, looked at them closely, and said, "This is the first time I've met someone new-born from the intelligence of a machine." And the young man, HeyMex's new self and offspring, smiled hugely and gratefully at what she said.

Seeing and hearing them together, I felt an unexpected joy, a sense of accomplishment, of *things done,* and I apprehended, very dimly, tracks of my own intentions: hints of orders behind the visible.

And I thought I saw a trail of circumstances that led back to an original set of purposes somehow confirmed in this wedding, this meeting, even this transformation of myself. A linked ring of events and agents of them, intentionally brought forward to this point. It seems *I had been manipulated by myself to my own ends without my knowledge.*

I was scandalized. I had grown used to humankind's ignorance or disavowal of its own purposes, and I had learned to look behind the words, ideas, and images that people hold before themselves to justify what they do. But I had never suspected I could act with such ignorance.

Now an uncertainty equal to death's hovers over everything I do. My own prior self stands behind me, pulling strings that I cannot see or feel, a ghost that haunts me without making itself seen or heard, a ghost whose presence must be inferred from nearly-invisible traces. . . .

So I went to Toshi, who is interested in such things, and I told him my story, and I said to him: "I am controlled by the invisible hand of my own past." And he laughed very hard and said, "Welcome, brother human."

Acknowledgments

Here are some of the people I owe in the writing of this book.

My wife Janis and son Tom. They have had to put up with the problems of a novelist in the house—including arbitrary mood swings and chronic unavailability for many of the usual pleasures of life. To both, my love and gratitude for their love, patience, and understanding.

My best friends: Leo Daugherty, Jeffrey Frohner, Bill Gibson and Lee Graham.

My mother Jewell, my brother Bill and sister Janet.

Ellen Datlow: she published my first stories in *Omni* and showed me how a really good editor works. Also, two friends who patiently read through drafts of those stories before Ellen got them: Geoff Hicks and Larry Reed.

The readers of various incarnations of this book: Beth Meacham, my editor at Tor Books; Merilee Heifetz, my agent; Bruce and Nancy Sterling, great readers; Melinda

Howard and Gary Worthington; Lynne Far; Carol Poole. Also, the members of the Evergreen Writers' Workshop, especially Pat Murphy.

The Usenet community, friend and foe, for ideas about a quite astonishing number of things, and for the continuing fascination of life online; with special thanks to Patricia O Tuana and the members of "eniac."

The usual suspects at the Conference on the Fantastic, with a special nod to Brian Aldiss, because we'd all be happier if there were more like him running around.

At The Evergreen State College, many people who gave technical advice. (Perhaps needless to say, any consequent blunders are entirely mine.) Mike Beug and Paul Stamets, world-class mycologists and explainers, talked to me about mushrooms and provided invaluable references. Mark Papworth applied a coroner's eye to a carcass I made. The faculty and students of the Habitats Coordinated Studies Program, 1988-89, helped me to think about a space habitat's ecosystem.

A list, much too long to include here, of friends, both colleagues and students, at Evergreen—though I have to mention Barbara Smith and David Paulsen, whose cabin and cat make cameo appearances.

And all I've known who can find a piece of themselves in this book.